"It would be a m⸺ of the word then?"

Shiloh felt her face flame. Lord, was she seriously considering his outrageous suggestion?

Cade gave her a slow nod, and the heat of desire crept into his eyes. "I'd like very much to make love with you," he confessed in a husky voice. "You have to know that I've wanted you since the first day you arrived."

She did know. She'd caught glimpses of her own need in Cade's eyes, but she'd been so guilty over what she considered her shameless sexuality that she'd convinced herself it was just her imagination.

"I'm in no hurry to consummate the marriage," he was saying now. "You have your baby and let your heart heal, and we'll go from there."

What more could she want?

Love, a small voice inside her said. *What about love?*

Dear Reader,

Welcome to Silhouette **Special Edition** . . . welcome to romance.

Last year, I requested your opinions on the books that we publish. Thank you for the many thoughtful comments. For the next couple of months, I'd like to share quotes with you from those letters. This seems very appropriate while we are in the midst of the THAT SPECIAL WOMAN! promotion. Each one of our readers is a *special* woman, as heroic as the heroines in our books.

Our THAT SPECIAL WOMAN! title for this month is *Kate's Vow,* by Sherryl Woods. You may remember Kate from Sherryl's VOWS trilogy. Kate has taken on a new client—and the verdict is love!

July is full of heat with *The Rogue* by Lindsay McKenna. This book continues her new series, MORGAN'S MERCENARIES. Also in store is Laurie Paige's *Home for a Wild Heart*—the first book of her WILD RIVER TRILOGY. And wrapping up this month of fireworks are books from other favorite authors: Christine Flynn, Celeste Hamilton and Bay Matthews!

I hope you enjoy this book, and all of the stories to come!

Sincerely,

Tara Gavin
Senior Editor

Quote of the Month: "I enjoy a well-thought-out romance. I enjoy complex issues—dealing with several perceptions of one situation. When I was young, romances taught me how to ask to be treated—what type of goals I could set my sights on. They really were my model for healthy relationships. The concept of not being able to judge 'Mr. Right' by first impressions helped me to find my husband, and the image of a strong woman helped me to stay strong."   —L. Montgomery, Connecticut

BAY MATTHEWS
WORTH WAITING FOR

Silhouette®

SPECIAL EDITION®

Published by Silhouette Books New York

America's Publisher of Contemporary Romance

For Jared Cade—my sixteen-month-old grandson, whose sleepy blue eyes and knock-'em-dead, show-us-your-teeth smile (à la Cade Robichaux) are sure to bring his parents grief. I love you, baby.

Thanks to Diane Wicker Davis, who, as usual, was a big help with her ever-listening ear, her astute criticism and her impeccable research and record-keeping.

SILHOUETTE BOOKS
300 East 42nd St., New York, N.Y. 10017

WORTH WAITING FOR

ISBN: 0-373-09825-1

First Silhouette Books printing July 1993

Printed in the U.S.A.

BAY MATTHEWS

of Haughton, Louisiana, describes herself as a dreamer and an incurable romantic. Married at an early age to her high school sweetheart, she claims she grew up with her three children. Now that only the youngest is at home, writing romances adds an exciting new dimension to her life.

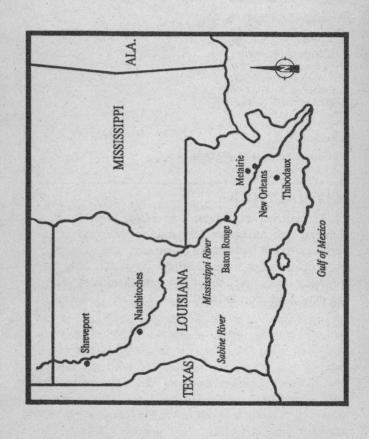

Chapter One

Shiloh Rambler stood just inside the doorway of the plush offices of the law firm of Delaney, Carver and Dempsey, her Gucci bag clutched against her breasts, her clear blue eyes focused on the man standing before her. He hadn't even offered her a chair.

A New Jersey transplant, Jack Delaney, the man she had known for ten months and who had been her lover the past three of those months, lounged against the corner of the polished ebony desk that reigned supreme over the elegant room. Jack might have been a part of the decorating scheme, so perfectly did he complement his surroundings. Like the room, he looked expensive and well tended, from his immaculate and perfectly tailored suit to his handcrafted Italian shoes.

As she stepped farther into the room, Jack crossed one foot over the other, burying the gleaming toe of his shoe in the thick pile of the smoke-hued carpet in an action that smacked of exaggerated nonchalance. He flicked an imaginary piece of lint from the sleeve of his suit.

"Well?" The imperious query was a perfect match for his chilling stare.

Something inside Shiloh shrank from that look, even though she hated herself for harboring any feelings for him after the way he'd thrown her love back in her face almost three agonizingly long weeks ago. Where was the smoldering desire those eyes had once held? Where was the tenderness? Where was the emotion she had convinced herself was love?

"Come, Shiloh," he said with a sneering lift of his shapely upper lip.

The sound of his voice reminded her that she was making him wait...something he abhorred. She brushed back a wisp of sable brown hair that clung to her cheek. "I needed to talk to you."

"Then talk. I haven't got all day. What's so damn important that you've badgered my secretary the last three days and threatened to make a scene in my office if I didn't agree to see you? Harassment is against the law, you know."

Was that a subtle threat? Touted by her brother, Garrett, as the epitome of the iron fist in the velvet glove, Shiloh preferred to win her battles with convincing smiles and undeniable logic rather than the steamroller tactics she'd been forced to use in order to gain admission to Jack's inner sanctum. His crass reminder of the actions so uncharacteristic of her turned the ivory complexion of her face hot pink.

Fighting the tears that had fallen with disheartening regularity since she'd last seen him, Shiloh squared her shoulders and allowed her gaze to climb from the front of his pristine white shirt to the sapphire hardness of his eyes.

"I apologize for that," she said, her voice trembling the slightest bit, "but if you had returned my phone calls, threats and harassment wouldn't have been necessary."

Jack's fair eyebrows drew into a straight, intimidating line. "Don't try to blame me for your behavior. I have no intention of taking responsibility for anyone's actions but my own."

Despite his coolness, Shiloh dared let a smidgen of hope surface. "Well, that's encouraging after the way you treated me the last time we spoke."

"Are you implying that I behaved irresponsibly during our relationship?" he asked, dashing the bit of hope before it could flourish.

Funny, she thought, she'd never noticed before how irritating his Yankee accent and his clipped tone were. "You led me on." It was more than a statement; it was an accusation.

"I showed you a good time."

"You made me believe you loved me."

His short bark of laughter grated on her tattered nerves. "I never said that I did. I wanted you. I was honest about that. In your naïveté you misconstrued my wanting to have sex with you with love."

Shiloh buried her teeth in the ripe fullness of her bottom lip, again fighting the sting of humiliating tears. Damn him! He knew exactly how to get to her. But then, he had from the beginning. "Maybe you're right," she told him, an insidious anger overtaking her feelings of inadequacy and rejection. "Maybe I am naive. At least it's better than being a pompous jerk."

Jack's mouth tightened, but he let the comment pass without retaliation. He stood and rounded the desk whose ebony expanse separated them as effectively as a moat, as surely as a barricade. "Get to the point," he said in an arctic tone. "I have more important things to do than rehash old affairs."

A fresh shaft of pain stabbed her heart. Even knowing that everything he'd said and done the past ten months had been a lie, classifying their time together as an affair hurt...almost as much as it had hurt when she'd realized how easily she'd been duped. Her chin rose to a defiant angle at the memory. She leveled a steady look into his eyes.

"I'm pregnant." The declaration fell like a wrecking ball into the silence of the room. The shock in Jack's eyes barely registered before she forged ahead. "I thought you had a right to know."

"Pregnant? How can you be pregnant?"

"It's a hazard of sex, Jack," she quipped in a tone that fell somewhere between flippancy spawned by anxiety and sarcasm born of disillusionment. "What are you going to do?"

"Do?" he echoed, even though it was obvious that his mind was elsewhere.

She combined a helpless smile, a shrug and a lift of her eyebrows. "Yes. What are you going to do about the baby—your being such a responsible guy and all?"

The comment, which he correctly interpreted as a deliberate dig, erased the glazed look from his eyes. The hardness came back. "What do you expect me to do? Tell you I made a mistake, that I love you and want to marry you and make a home with you for your little bastard?"

Shiloh gasped and recoiled a step at the cruelty of his remark. The pain and sickness washing through her made her feel as if she'd taken a blow to the stomach. "*My* little bastard?" she said in a voice that quivered with hurt and a rising anger. "What about you? Unless my memory fails me, you were there in the bed with me."

"Was I?"

The heated color of her anger drained from her face. Her blue eyes looked out of her pale countenance in utter disillusionment. "What's that supposed to mean?"

"You know what I'm getting at. How can I be sure it's mine?"

Shiloh swallowed back her growing nausea. She was shaking inside and out. "I can't believe you said that. For God's sake, Jack, it took you seven months to get me into bed. You know I don't sleep around."

Chagrin flickered across his handsome face, but his animosity returned with a vengeance. "Damn it, that's what you get for using something as outdated as a diaphragm. They went out with the Dark Ages."

"Why was I expected to take care of birth control? Why didn't it ever enter *your* mind?" she retaliated, stung by his insinuation that her pregnancy was her fault. "Condoms have been around since the Dark Ages, and they're just as popular and more effective now than they were back then."

"So I'm expected to share the guilt, is that it? Own up to my responsibility?"

Shiloh's blue eyes flashed with anger. "Well, if the Italian shoe fits—"

"Do you actually think I'm the kind of guy to stay at home and change diapers and have a squalling brat puke on me?'' he interrupted with a vehement shake of his tawny, well-groomed head. ''No way.''

For long moments Shiloh stared at his handsome face—the golden tan, the classic nose, the dark blue eyes surrounded by sinfully long lashes, the mouth that had driven her wild with longing. At that moment she knew that not only had she been a fool to believe him, she'd been a fool to believe that he possessed an ounce of sensitivity. He was a self-centered, egotistical slime. With a heavy heart and without a word she turned to leave.

''Wait!''

Feeling light-headed and empty inside, she turned to face him. He was bent over his desk, a silver-and-gold Mont Blanc fountain pen in his manicured hand. He finished writing with a flourish and brandished the rectangle of paper like a flag of truce. ''Take it. It's a check.''

''So I see,'' she said with admirable calmness considering that she was seriously weighing the consequences of ripping out his black heart with her bare hands. ''What are you trying to do, Jack? Buy me off?''

''Of course not,'' he scoffed. ''Look, you're alone. You can't want this baby. Take the money. Get an abortion and get on with your life.''

Shiloh had only thought she was angry before. Fury applied now. And rage. Red-hot and consuming. Clasping her purse to her chest, she closed her eyes, trying to calm herself. When she opened them again her blue eyes were about as calm as the sea before an approaching typhoon. In language that would have made a longshoreman proud, she told Jack Delaney just what he could do with his money.

"You ungrateful bitch."

Shiloh's bitter laughter was tinged with hysteria. "Ungrateful?" she said with a negative toss of her head. "Actually, Jack, I'm not. I'm very grateful. Grateful that I found out what you really are. Grateful that this baby will never have to know that the real bastard was his father."

"So you're going to have it?" He made "it" sound like a terrible disease.

Her smile was as brittle as ancient parchment. "You say to get on with my life. Well, I've got a news flash for you. Planned or not, this pregnancy *is* my life. I'm not getting any younger. These are the cards I was dealt, Jack. Like any Rambler, I've got to play them out. This may be my only chance to have a child, and I'm damn sure going to take it."

"What's your family going to say?"

"I'm an adult, capable of making my own decisions. If they don't approve—if *you* don't approve— it really doesn't matter."

"Isn't that attitude a bit selfish?"

"Selfish?" she echoed. Without a word she strode across the room to one of the bookshelves and pulled down a thick tome, which she dropped onto the desktop. It landed with a dull thud. "Here's a dictionary," she told him. "You really should look up the meaning of that word yourself."

She gave him a glance that consigned him to hell and turned for the door again. This time he didn't try to stop her. It was just as well. Her composure was good only for the time it took her to close the door with a jamb-shaking, soul-satisfying crash and make her way through the outer offices to the hallway. There her facade of composure crumbled, and the tears began.

Two hours later Shiloh sat propped against a pile of pillows in her bed, her eyes red rimmed from her crying and her nose as raw as her heart. Because of her parents' multiple marriages—four for her mother and five for her dad—she had vowed early in life to steer clear of any serious entanglements. The fact that her parents' marital scorecards reflected that they had married each other twice and were happily married at the present hadn't lessened her determination not to fall into that same trap herself.

During her high school and college years, Shiloh had adopted a love-'em-and-leave-'em attitude, littering Chattanooga with a trail of broken hearts, carelessly casting aside the young men who sought her heart and her hand before they had a chance to hurt her.

As she'd grown older she'd switched her focus. For the most part she'd set aside her personal life and concentrated on securing her future. She'd become a master chef and, armed with a considerable amount of money borrowed from her father, she had opened Le Mirage. The restaurant, which served the finest of French cuisine, had caught on quickly with the gourmets and gourmands of Chattanooga. She and her restaurant had become an instant hit.

Though her business life had thrived, her personal life was as barren as the Mojave after a ten-year drought. She became even more selective, never dating a playboy type more than a few times and marking men with divorces off her list completely. Though she had occasionally fallen prey to a healthy libido and convinced herself that what she'd felt during those rare and infrequent affairs was love, none had proved lasting.

She knew she was too particular, and she realized that one bad marriage didn't make a man a loser, but she had no intention of putting any children she might have through the same pain and disillusionment she and Garrett had suffered growing up. If and when she married, the man would be perfect. Deep in her heart she knew there was no such creature and that love didn't come with any guarantees, but the fears of a lifetime had turned caution into near paranoia.

At night, weary with the problems of business and listening to the inevitable ticking of both her bedside and her biological clocks, she admitted a soul-deep regret for the lack of love and affection in her life. The older she got, the more she realized that she not only craved the special closeness of a serious man-woman relationship, but that she needed it. Maybe she even needed the heartaches that seemed to go hand in hand with falling in love. She was tired of being alone, tired of being strong. She longed to lean on someone else for a change.

She didn't want to think of herself as desperate—God forbid!—but the day she'd celebrated her thirty-third birthday she knew that she'd reached a peak of vulnerability—which was why handsome, charm-your-pants-off Jack—who was two years older than she—had seemed so perfect. She'd met him on a scorching July afternoon as he was carrying boxes into an apartment down the way. Good-neighborlike, she'd offered to carry in some of his houseplants, and it was over an ice-cold cola that she had learned that he was single, that, in fact, he had never been married.

Rather than imagine some negative reason for his remaining unmarried for so long, Shiloh had looked upon his lengthy bachelorhood as a plus. She was positive that, like her, he was waiting for the right person and the right time before making a commitment for a lifetime.

Jack, who had moved to Tennessee six years before, was part of a thriving corporate law firm with offices in the best part of town, designed and decorated by the best interior designers in the country. He had claimed that he planned to use the same people to decorate his apartment, but after ten months unpacked boxes were still stacked in every corner.

He wore a Rolex nestled against the golden hair of his tanned wrist, drove an Alfa Romeo, worked out at a private gym and vacationed in places whose names reeked of romance: Kashmir, Barbados, Vienna. Everything about him exuded sex appeal and confidence.

He hadn't hesitated to admit that he was ambitious or that he'd worked long, hard years to get to his current place of prominence in the world of Chattanooga business and society, a place of prominence he intended to maintain, whatever it took. His admission hadn't sounded selfish to Shiloh. No stranger to ambition herself, she'd applauded his determination and complimented him for setting and meeting such high goals.

After their first meeting Jack had wasted no time making it clear he was interested in becoming more than neighbors, which had suited Shiloh just fine. By every outward appearance they were a matched set. She was Yin to his Yang, sugar to his spice, the reflection of his light. They liked the same music, the same movies, the same kind of architecture—the same kind of everything, it seemed.

Jack had pursued her with every weapon in his considerable arsenal: nights spent dancing beneath starry skies, daily bouquets of flowers of every description, Godiva chocolates, truffles flown in from Europe. Flattered and falling harder for him by the day, she'd still been wary about succumbing to his sexual advances and the feelings growing inside her. But despite her vows and fears she had been helpless to fight the promise of happiness reflected in his blue eyes and, in due time, her protective shell had crumbled like the walls of Jericho at the blowing of the trumpets.

It had taken seven months for her to feel certain that what he was offering her was real, seven months before she'd lowered her guard enough to let him make love to her, but deep inside her lonely heart she'd known that once he'd set about winning her, she hadn't stood a chance. Though it had troubled her to think that all her years of caution were for naught, giving in to her emotions after so long had been a nice feeling, a feeling to revel in and hold close when he left her alone in her solitary bed, her body aglow from his lovemaking.

Blinking back more of the threatening tears, she smoothed her palm over the crisp sheets, imagining Jack's head on the pillow next to hers. After so many years of caution, after waiting so long to fall in love, how could she have been so wrong about Jack?

The end had come so abruptly, so unexpectedly. They had made love for hours, and just as Jack was about to slip on his clothes and leave—he never stayed all night—she had pressed a kiss to his sweat-dampened chest and uttered the three simple words she'd never said to a man before, three words she'd been afraid to say. She reasoned that Jack must have been afraid to say them, too, since he'd never spoken a word of love.

But she'd been wrong. Dead wrong. Fear hadn't stopped him from saying he loved her. He hadn't said it because he *didn't* love her. She could still hear the coldness of his voice, could still see the way he had pulled away from her, both physically and mentally, as he'd told her in no uncertain terms that he didn't need her love, didn't want it.

She had listened to the words that signaled the end of their relationship—their affair, she reminded herself with a fresh rush of tears—and wondered if the dead feeling creeping through her was the way the men she had turned away in her youth had felt when she'd broken off with them. And, as she'd watched Jack dress and listened to him say that he had no intention of marrying her or anyone else, it had crossed her mind that maybe God was punishing her.

There had been tears, of course, torrents of them, but they hadn't moved him one iota. She'd watched his intractable back as he walked out of her bedroom and her life. For a long, lonely and miserable week she'd left messages on his answering machine at home; he'd never returned her calls. When she'd phoned his office, she'd been given the runaround by his secretary. In the evenings, from her window, she had watched him pull into his parking space and had considered beating on his door until he had to open it or explain to the neighbors. But she hadn't. As bedraggled as it was, the tattered remnant of her pride wouldn't permit her to air her dirty laundry to the world.

Accepting the erroneous premise that she had driven him away, she hadn't called him at all the second week. Then, five days ago, seventeen days after he had dropped out of her life, she'd been curled up with stomach cramps when it had occurred to her that she couldn't remember when she'd had her last period.

She had consulted her calendar and ascertained the mind-boggling truth: she should have started almost a month before. Forcing back the panic that threatened to erupt in a scream of denial, she had driven to the nearest pharmacy and purchased an at-home pregnancy kit that had produced a positive result. She was pregnant by a man who didn't care if she fell off the face of the earth.

Though she wasn't sure what telling him would accomplish, she had resumed her calling, assuming that he would want to know about the conception of their child. Jack had agreed to see her... finally. Their conversation, or confrontation, that afternoon had been the result. At least, she thought as she blew her nose for perhaps the hundredth time, she knew what kind of man Jack really was, which was no man at all. And she knew where she stood. Where she had always stood. Alone. ——

She'd found out something else, too. She didn't hurt anymore. The disgust and arrogance in Jack's eyes had gone a long way toward killing any tender feelings that might have remained when she'd stepped through the doors of his office. The condescension and coldness on his face as he'd offered her the money for an abortion had finished off whatever love was left.

Maybe it hadn't been real love. Maybe she had been dazzled by his charm and charisma. Maybe she'd been in love with love and not Jack at all.

And what does that make you, Shiloh?

Lonely. And vulnerable.

Desperate? A fool?

So what if she was a fool? Hordes of people had played the fool in the name of love. Though she was more cautious than anyone else in her family, she was still a Rambler, and Ramblers had never been afraid of taking a gamble—on love or anything else. If she was destined to lose the game of love, at least, as she'd told Jack, she was determined to play out the hand she'd been dealt.

Fresh tears filled her eyes and she dashed them away with her fingertips. She'd cried more tears the past two and a half weeks than she'd shed in her lifetime. Tossing a sodden tissue into the wastepaper basket by her bed, she promised herself that these would be the last tears she'd cry over the mess she'd gotten herself into.

She'd punished herself enough for falling for Jack Delaney. She was only human, and as susceptible to the wiles of an experienced man as the next woman. Jack Delaney wasn't worth the ten months she'd wasted on him or the tears she'd cried for what she'd at first felt was her loss. In retrospect, God had done her a favor by exposing Jack's true colors. Now it was time to let go of the past and plan for the future. A future that held a baby.

She was going to have a baby.

Shiloh raised her hands to her breasts that felt full and tender. She couldn't imagine a baby nursing at her breasts. She moved one hand to her flat abdomen and tried to think of it round and hard, tried to picture a child moving inside her. Impossible to imagine. And inconceivable to think that Jack's child was, at that moment, drawing sustenance from her body, that what had begun as an act of love—at least on her part—was changing, growing into a baby.

Reality moved in ruthlessly, bringing with it an unsettling barrage of questions. How could she manage a business with a baby? What *would* her family say? Would they rally around her and give her support, or would they be sick with mortification? And, for all her show of confidence to Jack, how did she really feel about being an unwed mother?

While she wanted this baby and intended to have it, she admitted to more than a little embarrassment and even shame over the fact that she'd gotten "caught." Being the recipient of questioning looks and having to explain herself wasn't an appealing scenario, and telling herself that having babies out of wedlock was the norm for movie stars and other people in the public eye didn't help.

The fact was that in spite of her well-constructed facade as a modern woman, she was an old-fashioned girl at heart, one who had always tried her utmost to live up to other people's expectations of her. Her nature precluded her making judgments about the way other people ran their private lives, but she was much harder on herself.

Dear God! This was the sort of thing that happened to sex-crazy teens, not to women who should know better! How on earth was she going to break the news to her parents and Garrett? In despair, she covered her face with her hands, but she didn't cry. She wouldn't expend another drop of emotion on the likes of Jack Delaney. He wasn't even worthy of her anger. It was time to move on.

She lifted her head and squared her shoulders. She wasn't certain how or when she'd break the news to her parents, but she knew that when the time was right she'd find a way. She'd always been a fighter, and the next few months would prove what she was really made of. As her grandmother Rambler would have said, she'd made her bed; she'd have to lie in it.

She had. She was. But it was a very lonely place to be.

Shiloh awoke the next morning feeling like Atlas with the weight of the world on his shoulders. She was thankful that she wouldn't have to face anyone. Maybe if she had another day to work on her attitude and practice her false, sunny smile she could fool everyone at the restaurant—everyone but Julie.

On Sundays Le Mirage was left in the capable hands of Julie Scott, Shiloh's manager, a divorcée with flaming red hair and two teenaged daughters to put through college. Julie, still licking the wounds inflicted by her former husband, was more of a workaholic than Shiloh. They'd become friends soon after Julie was hired, and each was well aware that the fast-paced world of the popular eating establishment helped fill the empty hours that loomed in their lives. Like an age-old tradition, Julie made an offer to buy the restaurant at least twice a year, though it was understood that neither of them took it seriously. Today Shiloh was glad she had her friend to fall back on.

In a to-hell-with-it mood, Shiloh fixed and devoured a country breakfast of ham, basted eggs, homemade biscuits, milk, gravy and grits. She sopped up a blob of butter with the last bite of her fourth biscuit and popped the flaky morsel into her mouth. No use worrying about calories, she thought with a grim smile. Morning sickness should hit any day.

Morning sickness aside, she had a great metabolism and had no trouble maintaining her weight. Garrett always said she could put away enough food for a prize fighter even though she wasn't any bigger than a gnat.

Her smile faded. Garrett. As a mixed-up, introverted child, she had always found Garrett to be her port in a storm, a situation that hadn't changed as they'd grown older. What would her big brother say about her carelessness . . . and her foolishness?

Unable to bear the thought of his being upset with her, Shiloh rose and cleaned up her breakfast dishes. She tried to read, tried watching television, but the hellfire-and-brimstone preachers made her feel as if a scarlet letter had been branded onto her forehead.

At midday, unable to help herself, she peeked out the window. Jack's car was there. She closed the blinds with a mild oath and went to the bedroom. If she went to sleep she could kill two birds with one stone: she could forget her dilemma, and she could while away the seemingly endless hours of the afternoon.

Shiloh was awakened by the shrill ringing of the telephone. Pushing her tousled hair from her face, she raised herself to one elbow and reached for the receiver. "Hello," she said huskily.

"Hey, sis," came her brother's cheerful voice. "What's goin' on?"

Don't ask. "Nothing much," she lied. "How about you?"

"We're all fine. Your favorite niece, the lovely Laura Leigh, is better than fine. She's wonderful."

Shiloh couldn't stop the smile that claimed her lips. "Laura is my only niece, Garrett," she reminded him.

"That's true," he admitted.

"How's Molly?"

Molly O'Connell Rambler was the daughter of the woman who had been Garrett and Shiloh's stepmother at one point. A stepmother who had taken Rambler's Rest away from their father in a highly publicized, extremely messy divorce. Thankfully, Molly had taken after her father instead of her scheming, grasping mother. In fact, Molly was the only person who'd been able to reach Garrett after his first disastrous marriage. When the two of them had married three years before, Rambler's Rest had once again come into Rambler hands.

"Mol's in pretty good shape for the shape she's in," Garrett said.

"Garrett!"

He laughed. "For a woman who's seven months pregnant, she's lookin' reeeal good," he drawled. "Too good, in fact. Every time I look at her, I want to take her to bed and keep her there."

Shiloh's heart gave a painful lurch at his reference to his sexual longings. "That's what got you into trouble in the first place, brother dear," she reminded him.

"Trouble? This isn't trouble. This is heaven. I even love her little round belly. Crazy, huh?" he said with a laugh.

Shiloh's hand slid to her own abdomen in an involuntary gesture. Sadness enveloped her. Garrett's enthusiasm over the arrival of his second child, his love for his wife and his contentment with his life was evident from the sound of his voice. "I don't think it's crazy at all."

"No? That's sweet of you." Garrett continued with his favorite topic. "She has enough vim and vinegar to drive a wooden man crazy," he said with a chuckle. "And she's so darn gorgeous. I swear, sis, Molly's more beautiful pregnant than most women are on any given day."

Shiloh felt another painful catch in the vicinity of her heart.

"Sometimes I think I can see the happiness radiating from her."

"It could be you and not the pregnancy that makes her happy, you know," Shiloh suggested.

"I hope I'm at least part of the reason," he said. "Either way, I look at her and I know what a damned lucky man I am."

Shiloh couldn't help comparing his attitude with Jack's. It must be wonderful to have a loving husband, one who *liked* a stomach rounded with child. Shiloh couldn't squelch a fleeting pang of jealousy for her brother's happiness. Though the ungenerous feeling passed in a heartbeat, it left a lingering depression.

"Shiloh?"

The sound of his voice dragged her troubled thoughts back to the conversation. "Yes?"

"You sound a little down. What's the matter?"

"Noth—"

"And don't say nothing," he interrupted. "I know better. Is the restaurant doing okay?"

"Everything at Le Mirage is fine."

"Then it must be Jack."

Though the two men had never met, Shiloh had told her brother and his wife about Jack. Garrett, typically brotherlike, had cautioned her to be careful. His feeling was that if a guy got to be thirty-six without ever marrying, there was something wrong somewhere. Typically brotherlike, he'd been right.

"You must be psychic," she said, injecting a lightness she didn't feel to her voice.

"Trouble?"

Shiloh sighed and prepared for the inevitable third degree. "We split up about three weeks ago."

"Want to talk about it?"

"Not really, but knowing you the way I do, I figure you'll hound me until you know every gory detail, so I figure I can save myself a lot of grief if I tell you now."

"Smart girl."

Shiloh heard the smile in his voice. She gave another dejected sigh. "You were right about him—and don't you dare say I told you so!"

"I wouldn't dream of it," Garrett said in a gentle voice. "What happened, babe?"

"When he found out that I . . . was serious, he informed me that he had no plans for love or marriage. Needless to say, I was a bit surprised, considering the rush he gave me."

"It sounds like he's one of those guys who can't commit."

"What do you mean?"

"Some guys go after a woman like gangbusters, but when she shows signs of wanting to make the arrangement permanent these guys start backing off like crawfish. They just can't make a commitment. Sometimes it's hard for them to finish things."

Shiloh thought of Jack's apartment with its stacks of unpacked boxes. "That sounds like Jack, all right."

"Why didn't you call and tell me?" he asked.

"I'm a big girl, Garrett. I don't need your shoulder to cry on."

"Big girls don't cry, huh?"

A hard edge crept into her voice. "Not anymore, they don't."

"Thatta girl!" Garrett crowed. "Don't get mad, get even! Find yourself another guy and send ole Jackie boy a wedding invitation."

A picture of herself nine months pregnant, marching down the aisle on the arm of a faceless man, flashed through her mind. "I don't think there are going to be any men for a while."

"Don't let this make you bitter, sis," Garrett warned. "You may not think so now, but someday you'll realize that this was for the best."

"I already know that." In spite of her best efforts, her voice broke. "The real Jack wasn't anything like the man who courted me for all those months. God, I can't believe I was so stupid."

"You weren't stupid," Garrett soothed. "He just slipped up on your blind side."

"Yeah, well, I won't let that happen again, I promise."

"Don't make promises you can't keep."

"Stop sounding like a big brother, Garrett."

They shared a second of laughter and the line became silent suddenly. "You okay, sis? Really?"

The tenderness in his voice was almost her undoing. She blinked back the tears she'd sworn not to shed. "I'm okay. Really."

"I love you. So does Molly."

"I know."

"If you can get away sometime soon, why don't you come down? Molly would love to have you, and it might do you good to get away for a week or two."

"And have both of you treating me as if a broken heart has turned me into an invalid? No, thanks!"

Garrett laughed. "There are worse things."

"Mmm, I suppose," she said, but she sounded doubtful.

"At least think about it."

"I will."

"Look, sis, I have a meeting with a potential crawfish buyer this evening, so I'd better go."

"Sure. Thanks for calling. Give Molly and Laura a kiss for me."

"Will do. Talk to you later, babe. Bye."

Shiloh listened to Garrett cradle his receiver and slowly did the same. Witnessing his happiness only underscored the loneliness that was eating away at her. As much as she loved him, she found herself wishing he hadn't called.

She got up, turned on the radio to an oldies station and decided to give her book another try. She did pretty well—only finding it necessary to read a page twice before she knew what it said—until an old song came on about one being the loneliest number in the world. Again the tears threatened; again she fought them off.

If one was a lonely number, maybe the solution to loneliness was to up the numbers, be around other people, she reasoned. But the thought of calling one of her friends was intolerable. Going to the restaurant held no appeal, either. As a matter of fact, she wasn't sure she could ever go to the restaurant and be around those laughing, cheerful people again. She just wanted to crawl into a hole and hide so that no one would know what a fool she'd been.

It might do you good to get away for a week or two.

Garrett's voice drifted through her mind. This time the idea held a certain appeal. A visit to Louisiana might be just what she needed. There were bound to be last-minute things that Molly needed to do before the baby came. Helping her sister-in-law would take her mind off her own problems.

Of course, Molly and Garrett *would* pamper her and treat her as if she had some dread illness. Which, on second thought, didn't sound as bad as it had a while ago. She was tired—physically, mentally, emotionally. She needed some time and distance away from Jack Delaney and her problems so that she could think things through and come to a decision about how she was going to handle the next few months and single parenthood. She needed to be around people who loved her so that she could start rebuilding the self-worth Jack's rejection had battered down.

Rambler's Rest was where womanizing, gambling, black sheep Jonathan Garrett Rambler I had found his love and his peace more than one hundred and fifty years before. It was where Garrett had found Molly. It was where she herself had gone each summer of her youth to spend some time with her father.

She'd always looked forward to those summers and dreaded going back to Tennessee and the structure and regimen of school and lessons—piano, ballet, art. The hot, humid, slow-moving days spent with her father and Garrett exploring the wonderful world of the plantation had seemed out of another time, a period to step back and see what was happening around her, to gain a new perspective. A way to forget the world she'd left behind.

Which was exactly what she needed. To forget. To find a new perspective, a fresh start. With a smile that bordered on excitement, Shiloh rose and went to the phone. Where better to do those things than the place where Ramblers had been starting over for more than a hundred years? She would go back to the plantation and hope that she, too, could find her peace and her rest.

Chapter Two

The following Saturday Shiloh flew into New Orleans International Airport and rented a car for her drive to the plantation, which was situated a few miles south of Thibodaux on the Bayou Lafourche.

When she'd called Garrett back the previous Sunday and told him of her change of heart, he'd been ecstatic. Now, as she drove along the familiar highway, she was glad she'd changed her mind. A rising sense of well-being swelled inside her. Though the plantation had never been a permanent home for her, her despair and pain lessened with each mile that took her nearer.

She'd been thrilled when Garrett married Molly. Pleased that the place that had played such a major role in her personal history was no longer out of bounds, she had visited Rambler's Rest often the past three years. Even so, none of her previous visits had ignited this feeling of excitement that bubbled through her veins, the same excitement she had experienced on coming to Rambler's Rest as a child with the whole summer stretching out before her.

As she turned onto the lane that led to the house, her lips curved into a smile. Garrett's rice-crawfish fields bordered both sides. By the looks of it, her brother's new endeavor was starting to pay off. She drove past the pecan grove, and there it was, sitting smack-dab in the middle of two hundred acres, its forest green shutters a smart contrast to the fresh coat of blinding white paint.

Her first sight of the house had never failed to impress. Nor did it today. Here was southern elegance in all its honest best. Rambler's Rest wasn't fancy or grand, but the riotous colors in the shrubs and flowers scattered around the grounds more than made up for it. The prim exterior spoke eloquently of the hardworking past and the staunch determination to hold on to what was left of that past, but the vibrant hues of the foliage scattered over the lawn that stretched all the way to the levee were somehow a reminder of the glory days when riverboats carried gamblers down the bayou. Now only outboards or pirogues navigated the lazily moving waters.

Near the highway, at the front of the lawn, roses dripped in lush abandon over ornate wrought-iron fencing. A horseshoe-shaped driveway of crushed shells was banded on both sides by towering, multi-trunked crape myrtles, creating a leafy archway to the house. Four brick pillars—two at each end of the driveway, each bearing a lion rampant—marked the entrances. The razor-sharp leaves of pampas grass undulated in the soft May breeze. In late summer they would sport feathery, cream-colored spikes that Molly likened to horses' tails.

Shiloh turned into the driveway. Shells crunched beneath the tires. As she closed the distance between the car and the house she could see that someone was sitting on the wooden steps of the front porch—a man and a child. The child was Laura, of course, but the man didn't look like Garrett. Even though he was sitting, he looked too broad, too tall.

She pulled in to the parking space at the front of the house, turned off the ignition and, gathering her purse, opened the car door. Though it was late afternoon and the surrounding trees protected the driveway from the relentless rays of the sun, the wave of humidity that assaulted her was like the slap of a wet washcloth. Shiloh pushed her sunglasses to the top of her head and started for the house, thankful she was wearing a cool cotton blouse and baggy walking shorts.

Garrett and Molly, both wearing wide grins and waving wildly, stepped through the wide front door and started down the steps. Shiloh's heart lurched at the sight of her sister-in-law's advanced pregnancy. Molly wore a floral-patterned, dropped-waist sundress whose hemline stopped just short of the white sandals that buckled around her dainty ankles. Wispy tendrils of red hair had escaped the confines of her haphazard ponytail and curled around her glowing face. Even without makeup, she managed to look stylish and beautiful. How long before her own pregnancy started showing and she was forced into maternity clothes?

From the corner of her eye she saw the man rise, Laura in his arms. Something about him looked tantalizingly familiar, but before she could put her finger on it Garrett had locked her in a bear hug and whirled her up off the ground in a circle. Molly and Laura laughed in delight.

"Put me down, you big buffoon!" Shiloh squealed, laughing herself. Garrett ignored the command and, in the split second that her gaze swung past the stranger, she saw that he, too, wore a half smile. The upward curving of his hard mouth carved lines from the edge of his nose to the corners of his mouth and etched crow's-feet at the corners of his smoky blue eyes. That smile stole her breath as effectively as Garrett's iron grip.

A feeling of déjà vu held her in thrall. She knew that she'd seen that smile many times before, and that her reaction to it was as normal as the sun's daily setting behind the stand of hardwoods to the west. The realization that she was aware of the stranger as a virile, handsome man sent a feeling of dismay sweeping through her. What kind of woman would react this way to one man while carrying the baby of a man she professed to love? Dismay turned to embarrassment and something akin to shame.

Garrett set her to her feet and, holding her shoulders in his big hands, planted a loud kiss on her cheek. "I swear, sis, you're not bigger than a minute."

The reference to her petite five-foot-one-inch height elicited her usual response—a jab of her elbow to his ribs—as she walked past him toward Molly. The two women smiled at each other and shared a hug. The hardness of Molly's belly pressing against her own flat stomach was disconcerting. Maybe coming hadn't been such a great idea, after all. Instead of diverting her thoughts from her own problems, being around Molly might serve as a constant reminder.

Determined to recapture the positive feeling that had kept her buoyed up since she'd decided to make the trip, she pressed a kiss to Molly's cheek and stepped back, smiling into her sister-in-law's eyes.

"You look great, Mol."

Self-consciously Molly tucked a fiery lock of hair behind her ear. "I look like a cow!"

"You look gorgeous," Garrett growled, sliding his arms around her from behind and planting a moist kiss on her neck.

"You Ramblers!" Molly scoffed with an indulgent smile. "If I didn't know better, I'd think you'd all kissed the Blarney stone."

"Wanna hug."

The soft plea drew everyone's attention to Laura, whose head with its mop of strawberry blond curls lay on the stranger's shoulder. Her chubby arms were clamped around his neck in a gesture of possessiveness.

"Of course you want a hug from Auntie Shiloh, Laurie, love," Garrett said. "Give her a big moochie."

Shiloh hardly heard and was only marginally aware that her niece leaned toward her. Unable to help herself, she allowed her gaze to drift up, over the V of tanned, hair-sprinkled flesh exposed by his short-sleeved knit shirt. His chin, which looked as if he needed a shave, was barely saved from blatant squareness. The line of his nose was strong and clean. Twin slashes delineated straight, dark eyebrows. Vivid blue eyes that drooped slightly at the outer corners were fringed with short, thick eyelashes. Those eyes looked back at her, remembrance and a smile dancing in their depths.

"Laurie wanna moochie."

The gentle reminder brought Shiloh's attention back to her niece. Laura's arms were outstretched. In order to take her, Shiloh had to move nearer to the smiling man. Close enough to feel the warm hardness of his chest against her hand as she slid them around Laura's plump middle. Close enough to smell the spicy scent of his cologne. Close enough to remind her that in spite of her pregnancy, she was still a woman.

To cover her mortification she buried her face in the warm, moist hollow of Laura's neck. A mistake. The heady aroma of an expensive male fragrance clung to the child.

"Shiloh," Garrett said, "you know who this is, don't you?"

Shiloh was compelled to raise her eyes to his again. At the clash of blue to blue, memory came rushing back. Of course he looked familiar! He wasn't a stranger at all. He had worked on the plantation every summer, hauling hay and doing odd jobs for her father. She'd first set eyes on him at the impressionable age of eight; she hadn't seen him since the summer he'd graduated from college. Cade Robichaux. She remembered that Garrett had said he'd gotten married. She remembered something else.

The news had broken her fifteen-year-old heart.

All those years ago it hadn't mattered who she "liked" or happened to be dating back in Chattanooga. When she came to Rambler's Rest her interest in any male except the one standing before her withered like a morning glory in the afternoon sun. Every summer, from the time she was eight until she was fifteen, she'd fallen in love with Cade Robichaux all over again.

To Cade she'd been just a kid, Garrett's little sister, but he'd always treated her with kindness and affection and, if she made up an excuse or plot that demanded his time, he'd given it to her gladly. For eight years it had been enough to keep her feeling alive from one summertime visit to the next.

For a child who had more stepparents than most kids had extended families, for an insecure child who felt torn between her loyalty to her mother and her love of her handsome father, for a child who'd grown up being bounced from Chattanooga to Louisiana and back again with the advent of each major holiday, her summer crush on Cade Robichaux had been the only constant in her life.

The memory of how much she'd relied on those feelings brought forth a rush of ancient insecurities. Her hold on Laura tightened. "Hello, Cade," she said as shyly as that long-limbed, awkward girl might have.

"Hello, Shiloh." His gaze traveled the length of her curvy, petite body in a look that said without words that the seven years' difference in their ages was of no importance, a look that said he liked the way she'd grown up. "You're lookin' great."

She hugged Laura even closer and was rewarded with a wriggle of protest. "Thanks," she murmured. Reminding herself that she was no longer a child with a crush but a grown woman with more than adequate social skills, she asked, "What are you doing in these parts?"

"I live just down the bayou," he said, surprising her with the news.

The easy melody of his Cajun accent wrapped itself around her like a warm blanket. His "I" sounded like "ah," and the dropped *g*'s gave his words a sort of slurred softness that reminded her of those long-ago afternoons spent roaming the plantation and whiling away the hours in make-believe fantasies of pirates and riverboat gamblers. She hadn't realized how pretty the accent was, or how different it was from Jack's clipped tones.

"I'm planning a business dinner," he explained, "and stopped by to see if Molly could cater it for me."

"Oh." What kind of business? Shiloh wondered. It was hard to imagine bare-chested, Wrangler-clad Cade at a business function.

"Look, I know you two have a lot of catching up to do," Molly said, waving a hand before her heat-flushed face, "but can we finish this conversation inside?"

"I didn't realize you were expecting company," Cade apologized. "I really should go."

"Shiloh's not company," Garrett said, urging the group up the steps. "She's family."

"Come on, Cade," Molly insisted. "I have a pitcher of fresh-squeezed lemonade in the refrigerator."

Cade looked from Molly to Shiloh. "Okay," he said. "If you're sure I'm not intruding."

Shiloh wasn't even aware that she'd been holding her breath until it left her body in a soft whoosh of air.

"Of course you aren't intruding," Garrett said, holding open the screen door.

Molly wanted them to adjourn to the parlor like civilized folks, but Garrett said he'd rather they sat in the kitchen so that he could help her with dinner while they were all visiting.

"You'll stay, won't you, Cade?" Molly asked, setting a frosty glass of lemonade in front of him.

Cade glanced at the no-nonsense watch strapped around his brawny wrist. He wasn't wearing a wedding band.

"I'd love to, Molly, but I have a meeting with an electrician in an hour or so."

Though her curiosity was piqued about his marital status, Shiloh tried to deny that the feeling sweeping through her at the thought of his leaving bordered on downright disappointment. "Electrician?"

Cade nodded. "I just bought a place that needs extensive renovation."

"A place!" Garrett hooted. "You didn't buy a place. You bought a piece of history." He looked at Shiloh and lifted his eyebrows. "Magnolia Manor."

Shiloh couldn't hide her surprise. Magnolia Manor's history had been intertwined with Rambler's Rest for years, ever since the first Jonathan Garrett Rambler—Nate—had won the plantation from the original owner, Conrad Krueger, in 1852. What Nate didn't know when he went to inspect his new acquisition was that Krueger had committed suicide and left not only a crumbling estate but four orphaned children. When Nate married Lisette Antilly and moved to Rambler's Rest, he gave the plantation to Krueger's oldest son. Magnolia Manor had remained in Krueger hands until the Second World War, when two Krueger sons had been killed and the father had followed with a stroke. The grieving widow had sold the plantation to some upstarts from Ohio and moved to Baton Rouge.

"Magnolia Manor!" Shiloh was impressed. "How on earth did you buy Magnolia Manor?"

A dull flush spread over Cade's lean, whisker-stubbled cheeks, but he met her gaze without flinching. "I got a loan at the bank."

Only when she saw his discomfiture did Shiloh realize that he'd misunderstood what had motivated the question. At thirteen, when Darwin Robichaux had deserted his wife and three kids, Cade had inherited the role of man of the house. He'd worked at any odd job he could find to put a dollar in his pocket to help support his ailing mother and two sisters. The Cade Robichaux Shiloh had known was so poor that he could barely make ends meet, much less buy a plantation.

She felt her face flame. "What I meant was that it isn't every day a place like that comes up for sale."

Cade had the grace to look embarrassed. "No, it isn't," he agreed. "As for the electrician—you know how much it costs to keep one of these places up."

"I can imagine."

"A bundle," Garrett intoned from his station at the triple sink.

"The owners got tired of the constant drain, moved off and left it to the vandals. I stopped by one day when I was out driving and took a look around. Someone had been storing hay inside. I thought it was a crying shame that a place like that should be used for a barn, so I decided to see if they'd sell." He shrugged. "They did, and now I'm up to my armpits in renovations."

"It sounds exciting," Shiloh said, her imagination fired up. She'd always dreamed of fixing up an old house like Rambler's Rest.

"Sometimes," he said with a nod. "But so far all I've had are headaches. It's hell trying to make a house like that convenient to live in and still retain its integrity."

"I'm sure it is." Surprised by her eagerness to learn more about Cade's past, she leaned back in her chair with a smile. "So what else have you been up to? I know you got married."

"And divorced…about sixteen years ago," he told her.

"I'm sorry."

A cloud shadowed his blue eyes. "So am I."

"Do you have any children?"

He looked down at the little girl who had crawled back into his lap and curled up in total contentment. Shiloh imagined that she saw a fleeting glimpse of sorrow in his eyes. "Two. Jared is almost nineteen, and Sunny is going on sixteen."

Shaking off the appearance of despondency, he twined one of Laura's coppery curls around his finger and looked at Shiloh with a wry smile. "As for what I've been up to…I guess you could say I play video games all day."

"You what!"

Cade laughed. Like his voice, the sound of his laughter was low and warm and sent a shiver of awareness scampering through Shiloh.

"I write video games," he explained. "You know, like for Game Boy, Nintendo—that sort of thing."

"You're kidding," she said, then, fearful that he'd misunderstand again, she added, "I mean, you were always such an outdoors type."

"Yeah, well, I learned to use my head instead of my hands."

Thinking about how his youthful body had glistened with sweat as he'd hoisted hay onto the flatbed trailer, Shiloh sighed. "That's a shame," she said with a touch of wistfulness.

"I beg your pardon?"

Realizing that her memories threatened to get her into trouble, she started crawfishing. "I mean, it's a real shame about your marriage . . . with the kids and everything."

"It happens," he said. "Sometimes despite everyone's best efforts, people fail each other."

Maybe so, but she couldn't imagine Cade not succeeding at anything he attempted. She recalled her own recent failure with Jack. "Yeah, I guess they do."

"What about you?" he asked. "What does Shiloh Rambler do for a living?"

In the conversational limelight, she felt like a confused adolescent again—awkward, unsure of herself. . .as if she'd gambled on some huge stake and lost. The gloss of sophistication she'd worked so hard to polish had been trampled in the dust of Jack Delaney's desertion.

From the corner of her eye she caught Garrett's considering look. She couldn't let him know what a number Jack had done on her. He'd be disappointed in her lack of spunk. *She* was disappointed in her lack of spunk. Determined not to let Jack Delaney rob her of anything else, determined to enjoy this time with an old acquaintance, she raised her chin to an angle just shy of obstinate and said, "I'm a master chef. I own my own restaurant."

"Well, you don't have to be so defensive about it," Cade said with a grin. He lifted his wide shoulders in a shrug. "I mean, it's hard to believe that you can actually cook, but who am I to judge?"

Shiloh recognized his teasing manner from her youth. Cade and Garrett had loved to bait her. She'd hated it, but loved it. It meant she had their undivided attention, something she seldom got from anyone. She realized with a bit of a start that she'd missed that masculine teasing. Now that she'd grown up and her father looked upon her as an equal, they often shared lighthearted banter. And Garrett, of course, still taunted her with annoying regularity. But Jack hadn't known the meaning of the word. Jack Delaney gave the word *uptight* new meaning. It was nice sharing the good-natured teasing with Cade.

"You mean it's about as mind-boggling as your using your head instead of your hands, huh?" she countered with a smile.

"Just about," he admitted, "considering I still carry a vivid recollection of your early cooking efforts."

"What early efforts?"

"You don't remember the oatmeal cookies you made for us hay hands that summer?" He frowned thoughtfully. "You must have been about ten."

"Lord, I remember!" Garrett piped up. "What a disaster!"

"Garrett!" Molly chided.

"Well, hell, babe, the recipe called for a teaspoon of cinnamon and she put in a tablespoon. Dad and I had heartburn for two days."

Everyone laughed, even Shiloh. "Let me assure you, I've honed my culinary skills."

"Then get up here and prove it," her brother urged.

"I'm on vacation," Shiloh reminded him and went back to her reminiscing with Cade. Over the next several minutes, during which Laura got bored and went to her room to play, Shiloh learned that Cade's mother had died four years before, her weak heart finally giving up the battle. His sisters were well: Monique was married and had three kids, and Chantal was divorced and in hotel management.

Shiloh talked about her business and revealed that she'd never been married. She hoped he didn't sense the tenseness that gripped her as she made the admission, hoped he bought the flip manner in which she delivered it. And she prayed that the disgust she felt toward herself and Jack wasn't evident in her tone or her eyes.

All too soon, Cade was rising and stretching his broad-shouldered, six-foot-two-inch frame. Shiloh didn't understand the feeling of disappointment that filled her. It had been an enjoyable hour. She watched as he went to the sink and dropped a kiss to the top of Molly's burnished copper head.

"Thanks for the lemonade, Molly. I'll give you a call later about the dinner."

"Sure you can't stay?" Molly pleaded.

He shook his head. "Maybe next time." He shot Shiloh a teasing glance. "Let me know what night Shiloh's cooking, and I'll make it a point to be here."

Garrett pointed the fork he was using to turn the chicken at his friend. "You're on."

"Maybe I won't cook while I'm here," Shiloh said.

"You'll cook, or I'll send you back to Tennessee," Garrett threatened. To Cade he added, "Her crepes are to die for."

"I can't wait." Cade turned to Shiloh and held out his hand. Shiloh wanted to cling to the strength and warmth of the fingers that curled around hers. "It was great seeing you," he said, his eyes clear and full of well-remembered tenderness. "You've grown into a very lovely lady."

"Thanks. You've held up pretty well yourself."

Cade placed a hand over his chest, as if the good-natured dig had pierced his heart. "Not bad for an old guy of fortysomething, huh?"

"Almost forty-one, isn't it?"

His lips curved into a wry smile. "How tacky of you to remember."

Everyone laughed, and Molly walked him to the door amid chorused goodbyes. Shiloh watched him leave and felt an acute poignancy squeeze her heart. Tapping the root of the feeling wasn't hard. She was sorry for not keeping in touch, sorry for the bad things that had happened to him. On the other hand, coming back and seeing him was like running into an old and valued friend.

She tried to ignore the chanting of her heart that told her that she was fooling herself, that the bitter-sweet feeling she was experiencing had nothing at all to do with old friendship and more to do with the fact that the Cade Robichauxs of the world were so few and far between and always out of her league.

Cade, who left Rambler's Rest with Shiloh Rambler's beauty uppermost on his mind, would have been amused and surprised to know that she considered him out of her league, when in reality it had always been the other way around. He got into his Bronco and started the seven-mile drive to Magnolia Manor, reflecting on his unexpected meeting with Shiloh and pondering the rush of memories triggered by her presence, memories he thought he'd left in the past.

Though he wasn't bitter over it, he'd always known that he was the kid from the wrong side of the tracks, the boy not good enough for the likes of Ramblers and Kruegers, a theory borne out when Darwin Robichaux had run out on his family.

He was just thirteen when his father, the equivalent of the town drunk, had deserted his family. The acid of bitterness had etched the details of the March day deep into Cade's brain. He had come home from school to find out that his dad was gone, that his mama had taken a bad turn and that there wasn't a penny in the house for her medicine. It was the same day the power company had turned off the electricity and what meager food was left in the old refrigerator was lukewarm and well on its way to ruination.

The recollection spawned a burst of anger, and Cade ground the Bronco's gears as he slowed to make a turn onto the highway. Just like that, he'd found himself thrust into the role of family provider. If he lived to be a hundred he'd never forget the helpless, hopeless looks on his sisters' faces when they asked him what they were going to have for supper. If he lived to be a thousand he'd never forget the sorrow in his mother's eyes as, from the depths of her sickbed, she apologized for Darwin's negligence.

He remembered that first night clearly. For supper he'd fixed macaroni and cheese—made with government cheese and powdered creamer mixed with water instead of milk—and opened a can of pork and beans. They'd eaten by candlelight and, for his sisters' benefit, he'd pretended he was a waiter in a fancy French restaurant where it was chic for diners to dine by the soft glow of candles. They'd bought it, and the next day he'd gone begging to the electricity company, telling them of his dad's desertion and his mother's illness. They'd gone out that very day to turn the lights back on, and he'd paid them every penny owed—a dollar or two at a time.

The next day he'd known he had to get a job. He'd tried almost everywhere, but everyone told him he was too young. For days he had pestered Mr. Renard at the drugstore until he'd agreed to let him clean up after hours in exchange for his mother's heart medicine.

His mama was taken care of, but they still needed money to live on. When she improved, Hattie and eight-year-old Chantal started taking in ironing. Eleven-year-old Monique baby-sat and cleaned houses. Cade got an early-morning paper route, rising at five and throwing papers from his ancient bicycle onto the porches of houses he would give his pinkie to see the inside of. Mornings and afternoons were spent running errands for the elderly and mowing yards until the rickety mower he was using leaked out all the oil and ruined the engine.

The haunting images of the past brought a burning pain to Cade's gut and an ache to his heart. No matter how hard they had worked, their combined incomes had never been enough for anything more than the necessities.

One morning in early June he'd heard that Jon Rambler needed people to work the hay fields at Rambler's Rest. Desperate, he had hitchhiked to the plantation. Claiming to be fifteen, figuring God would forgive him since it was for a good cause, he had asked Shiloh's dad for a job. His size and his air of quiet determination had made the lie believable, and Jon had hired him on the spot.

Cade smiled at the memory. It had been three years before Jon had learned that Cade had lied about his age. By that time Cade had made himself indispensable around the plantation. Jon had put him on a weekly salary and lent him an old truck to drive, telling him that a man shouldn't have to be dependent on anyone for transportation. In exchange for Jon's kindness Cade had hauled hay, repaired fence, worked on the farm equipment, painted, weeded and done anything else that needed doing.

Jon Rambler and his children had become Cade's extended family. Though there were a few years' age difference between him and Garrett, Cade thought the younger man had a lot of sense. And unlike the polished woman he'd seen today, Cade remembered Shiloh as a quiet child with long, coltish legs and fine brown hair that was forever escaping the rubber band used to bind it and straggling down around her wide-eyed face.

Like any little girl with time to waste and no friends to play with, she'd tagged after her brother from dusk till dark. Garrett, who confessed to feeling sorry for her, took it in stride. Cade felt sorry for her, too. It was obvious that she adored her father, and also obvious that Jon had no idea what to do with her. To ease her pain and perhaps his own, Cade found himself answering her endless questions and, if time permitted, helping her with her current pastime, whether it was catching butterflies or collecting pretty rocks.

Remembering her curvaceous body and pretty face, Cade found himself wondering if, as an adult, she collected hearts. She'd said she was single, and knowing her as he had, he couldn't see her giving her heart away easily. After all, he'd been a witness to her emerging independence. By the time she'd reached her teens, her armor of subtle sarcasm was firmly in place. Having developed his own armor through the years, he'd recognized it for what it was—a way to keep from being hurt. He had respected her for it and protected her whenever he could, for as long as he could.

He chided himself for letting his thoughts dwell on Shiloh Rambler and the past. She was only here for a short visit and, even though she'd been friendly and he'd like to think that the difference in their ages and social status no longer mattered, he was crazy to think that she'd ever give him a second thought.

Cade turned into the lane that had once bisected acres of ripening sugarcane. Now the land was planted in coastal Bermuda grass that, when properly cared for, could be cut every thirty-five days for hay. He passed the crumbling remains of a partially finished sugar mill and the decaying remnants of the slave quarters, one of which had been kept in good enough repair that he'd been able to renovate it for an office.

He and the carpenter thought the dovecote might be salvageable, but the greenhouse had become a target for vandals, and more glass had been shot out than was intact. He turned into the driveway at the back of Magnolia Manor and pulled the vehicle next to the hitching post where Nate Rambler had once tied his horse.

Turning off the Bronco's engine, he went inside and found that the carpenters had gone for the day. He went into the kitchen—one of the few finished rooms and the only one to house any modern appliances—and reached into the refrigerator for a cold beer. Unable to shake the picture of Shiloh Rambler from his mind, he wandered out onto the lower *galerie* and succumbed to his unending fascination for the slow-moving bayou.

After he'd graduated from Thibodaux High School with the third-highest GPA in the class, Cade had taken advantage of his scholarship to Northwestern University in Natchitoches, receiving a degree in computer science and specializing in computer programming. For a kid who'd grown up using his brawn instead of his brain, his natural aptitude for the computer had been a welcome surprise.

Though he'd been away during the school year, he'd spent holidays and summers with his family and working at Rambler's Rest. Besides the love of his mother and sisters, it had been the only thing he could count on... until he met Mary Rose Beaufort, the Methodist preacher's niece. Mary Rose was pretty and sweet and loved being with him. He'd loved being with her, too—even though her constant devotion was a bit confining.

The day before his college graduation had been another memorable day in his life. Mary Rose had come to him in tears, telling him she was pregnant. He'd been overwhelmed, devastated, but ready to do the right thing. Though the news was hardly joyous—all Cade could see was two more mouths to feed—he'd promptly offered to marry her. There was no way he'd desert his child the way Darwin had.

He and Mary Rose were married in her uncle's home—Cade in a suit borrowed from Jon Rambler and Mary Rose in a white linen suit from J.C. Penney, paid for by her aunt and uncle. Jon's gift to his loyal worker was a check for a hundred dollars and a set of crystal glasses that Mary Rose managed to break the first year.

Despite the fact that he hated the city, Cade got a job working in the computer division of General Dynamics in Fort Worth and moved his new bride there. His son, Jared, was born seven months after the wedding ceremony—Jon sent a bassinet—and Sonia, better known as Sunny, had come along three years later.

Cade had spent a lot of time working after hours, and every hour not spent at his regular job was spent developing games for the video market, the result of a contact he'd made through a friend of a friend of Jon Rambler's. He stashed away this extra money in savings. Even now he could recall his numbing weariness, but it hadn't mattered how tired he got. He wanted his family to have things he hadn't. He didn't want them to be looked down on. Someday, he vowed, he would be recognized as someone besides Darwin and Hattie Robichaux's brat.

As many plans do, Cade's had gone awry. His marriage had broken up weeks after Sunny's birth. Mary Rose, who had expected him to be her emotional support as well as her breadwinner, had decided that she couldn't stand playing second fiddle to his computer.

She had packed up and moved back to Thibodaux, taking the children and a goodly portion of Cade's self-worth with her. Despite the money in the bank, of which he gave generously to his children, he had felt like a complete failure. Craving the love he felt had somehow passed him by, he'd gone through a succession of meaningless relationships. Still empty, needing something he couldn't put his finger on, he had thrown himself into a new project that combined his love of history—especially the Civil War—and his knowledge of computer programming.

The result was a series of war games that was snapped up by one of the biggest video companies in the country. The games were an instant success. So was Cade. Money came in faster than he could figure out what to do with it, and his name was talked about in all the right circles. Nearly seven years ago, nine years after his divorce, he felt he was financially able to quit his regular job and move back to Thibodaux. Even though the folks of Thibodaux and Houma had a hard time believing that Darwin and Hattie Robichaux's son was so smart or so rich, it was hard *not* to believe when he bought a house on forty acres and a new Jeep Cherokee. Not only had he become an overnight celebrity, he was now considered quite a "catch" by the local singles crowd.

A catch. Ironic, really. If he was such a damn good catch, why was he single? Why was he so alone? Beer in hand, Cade went inside, prowling the partially finished rooms of the old house, the crowning symbol of his success. The electrician would be arriving at any moment, and Cade would be glad to have someone to talk to.

During the day, while he was working, the loneliness wasn't so bad. But when the workers left and he went room to room to check on the progress, the sound of his boots echoing hollowly through the high-ceilinged rooms seemed to mimic the aching hollowness of his heart.

It didn't make sense, he thought, downing a mouthful of the yeasty brew. He had everything he'd ever dreamed of and wanted—didn't he? Money enough to live on *and* for a rainy day. A house with a hundred-and-fifty-year-old history. His children—good kids by anyone's standards—lived nearby; what else could he possibly desire?

Love, maybe. Not much to ask for, but impossible to find, it seemed. Despite his love for his kids and his efforts to be a good father, Cade didn't fool himself. He was not close to Sunny and Jared. The nine years he'd spent in Fort Worth, seeing them only during the summers, had left a chasm between them that he wasn't sure how to bridge. Sometimes, when he was at his lowest, he even contemplated the idea that Jared's and Sunny's love for him was directly connected to what—and how much—he could offer them.

He sighed and swallowed the last of the beer. His thoughts were familiar territory, ground he covered almost daily, without finding answers. The truth of the matter was that he was as lonely as hell, and it seemed to have gotten worse since he'd moved into Magnolia Manor. Since moving into the old house that had once held a close-knit family, he'd realized that he'd been so busy securing his future that he'd done a disservice to Mary Rose and the kids and even himself. He had let life—and love—pass right on by.

The doorbell rang, shattering his dark musings. Setting the perspiring can on top of the gleaming, re-furbished mantel, he strode to the door, wondering, in retrospect, if the price he'd paid for his success was too steep after all.

Chapter Three

After finishing a meal of southern fried chicken with all the trimmings, Molly and Shiloh cleaned up the dinner dishes while Garrett put Laura to bed. Shiloh's troubled thoughts were centered on her chance encounter with Cade Robichaux and her unexpected awareness of him.

As if she could read Shiloh's mind, Molly asked, "He's nice, isn't he?"

"Hmm?" Shiloh said, drying a stainless steel pan with abstracted thoroughness.

"Cade."

At the mention of the man who had snared her thoughts, Shiloh's attention jumped to her sister-in-law.

Molly hung up her dish towel. "Welcome back. You've been staring off into space for the last five minutes, drying dishes on automatic pilot."

"I was woolgathering," Shiloh confessed. "It doesn't take a lot of mental energy to dry dishes." She deposited the last pan into the cavernous drawer beneath the stove top. "Did you say something about Cade?"

"That he's nice. Darn handsome, too."

"He always was," Shiloh agreed. Striving for nonchalance, she asked, "Does he come over often?"

"Fairly often," Molly said, switching off the light and leading the way to the parlor. "He works long hours, but he stops by at least once a week. He and Garrett renewed their acquaintance after Garrett and I got married, and they've grown into pretty good friends." She grimaced. "Garrett is always trying to fix him up with some woman or another."

"He isn't seeing anyone?" Shiloh asked, unaware that the wistful note in her voice reflected more than casual interest.

"No one in particular. A lot of women would like to get their claws into him, but so far he's evaded the altar."

"Maybe he still cares for his wife."

"Mary Rose?" Molly shook her head and lowered her bulk into a corner of the Victorian sofa. "I don't think so. Mary Rose remarried a couple of years after the divorce, and as far as I can see she's as happy as a fat hog in the sunshine. She and Cade have an amicable divorce, and he truly doesn't act like a man carrying a torch."

Shiloh laughed, her tip-tilted nose crinkling in delight. "You Louisianians certainly have a way with words."

"So I've been told," Molly quipped, swinging her feet onto a tapestry-covered footstool with an audible sigh.

Shiloh looked at her sister-in-law and envied the bloom of happiness on her face. Garrett was right. She glowed with health and a beauty that went far beyond the superficial. Was it the pregnancy alone? She didn't think so. It was being content in the knowledge that you were loved and cherished. Shiloh felt a tightness gather in her throat.

"Has anyone told you that you look marvelous for someone seven months pregnant?"

"Just my husband—" Molly held up her thumb and index finger with a quarter inch of air between them "—who could be just the teeniest bit biased." She raised one foot. "Good Lord, would you look at those ankles?"

They were swollen. "It's all right, isn't it?" Shiloh asked, concern lending an edge to her voice. "I mean, is it serious?"

Molly shook her head. "I've been retaining water lately. I did with Laura, too. They'll be fine by morning."

Shiloh wondered what surprises, besides swollen ankles, the next few months might hold for her. She knew she should go to the doctor and have her pregnancy confirmed. She should have gone before coming to Louisiana, but she hadn't been able to gather up the nerve. Promising herself she'd go as soon as she got back to Chattanooga, she asked, "Does it bother you?"

"What? Swollen ankles?"

Shiloh shrugged. "That. All of it. Losing your figure, running to the bathroom every ten minutes, the labor...everything."

"Sometimes," Molly admitted with a smile that more resembled a grimace. "Especially during those last days when I resemble a beached whale and Garrett has to help me out of the bathtub. Fortunately only the stretch marks are permanent, and I only had a couple of little ones around my belly button after Laura was born. At my normal size, you can't even see them." She crossed the fingers of one hand and lovingly smoothed the mound of her stomach with the other. "I don't think I have any new ones with Bubba here."

"You're sure it's a boy?"

"As sure as we can be with an ultrasound."

Shiloh was thoughtful a moment. For the first time she wondered what her baby would be. Would she want to know? "Does knowing what you're having take all the excitement out of it?"

"Not really. If I want excitement, I just look at my husband. He's ecstatic. Of course, what man wouldn't be ecstatic over having a son?"

Jack Delaney, Shiloh thought. Would knowing he was having a son have made a difference in Jack's reaction to her pregnancy? Doubtful. From what she had learned about Jack, it was doubtful that anything could rock his self-centered universe. But while the thought of having a son probably wouldn't affect Jack, the thought of it brought a surge of panic and inadequacy to Shiloh. How could she raise a son alone? She knew nothing about boys.

"Are you okay?"

Again, Molly's words intruded on Shiloh's thoughts. "What?"

"Are you okay? You've been sort of...distracted ever since you got here."

"I'm fine," Shiloh said with a smile as false as Jack Delaney's feelings.

"Are you sure?" Molly pressed. "I don't want to pry, but Garrett told me about you and Jack. If you want to talk..." Her voice trailed away momentarily. "Sometimes it helps."

The urge to tell Molly about the baby was strong, but the possibility of confronting her shock was more than Shiloh was up for at the moment. There was plenty of time. Months, in fact, to break the gruesome news.

"It's not a new story. He made me think we were perfect for each other and that he was crazy about me. He made me fall for him, and then, when I told him how I felt, he dumped me."

"The creep," Molly said, in true sisterly fashion.

"I should have listened to Garrett. He told me all along that something was wrong with Jack."

"Honey, Garrett would find something wrong with any man you wanted to marry. You know how families are. No one is ever good enough."

Shiloh smiled and thought of Garrett's reaction to her past beaux. "You're right. He is hard to please. Poor little Laura."

"He's already threatening to put her in a convent," Molly said, tongue-in-cheek.

Shiloh grinned. "That sounds like my big brother."

"What sounds like me?"

"Nothing!" the two women chorused in tandem, and, meeting each other's smiling gaze, they began to laugh.

"Never go up against two women," Garrett said with a shake of his head.

"Smart guy," Molly said. "Is the baby asleep?"

Garrett sat cross-legged on the floor and began to rub Molly's puffy feet. "She's bathed, in bed and had *Green Eggs and Ham* read to her twice. She was nodding off when I came down."

"Speaking of which, I think I'll go up," Shiloh said, rising. "I'm bushed."

"Traveling is always tiring," Molly sympathized. "Sleep in tomorrow. There's nothing much going on."

"I may just do that." Shiloh gave her brother and his wife a hug and started for the stairs.

"Sleep tight and don't let the bedbugs bite," Garrett called softly, recanting the nighttime chant from their childhood.

"You, too," Shiloh called back.

Garrett watched his sister ascend the stairs. "She looks tired."

"I know the trip was tiring, but it's as much what she's going through mentally as it is a physical weariness."

Garrett leaped to his feet. "That Delaney bastard ought to be hanged!"

"I agree, honey, but it happens every day." Molly reached for Garrett's hand. Her eyes were filled with understanding and strength. "Your sister is one of the strongest women I know. She'll get over him."

The words took the wind from the sails of Garrett's anger. He sat beside Molly and stroked his index finger down the creamy flesh of her cheek. The gentle gesture belied the tortured emotions in his eyes. "Yeah, but at what price? You know how careful she's been, how hard it is for her to give away her feelings. Deep in her heart she must have believed this bum was the real thing."

"I'm sure she did."

There was nothing else to say. After long moments of silence Garrett asked, "Do you really think she'll get over him?"

"Of course she will. It may take time, but she'll find someone else, someone decent and good."

"There aren't many of that breed out there."

Molly smiled and twisted the button of his shirt. "Oh, there are a few left. I'd hate to think I got the last one."

Garrett drew her head to his chest. "Do you think she was glad to see Cade?"

Eyes closed, Molly snuggled closer. "She seemed to be. Why?"

"No reason," Garrett said with a shrug. "I thought they had a good visit." A sly smile crossed his mouth. "Did you see how he was looking her over?"

"I really didn't notice," Molly replied.

"I did." Satisfaction laced Garrett's voice. He gave a lazy nod and rubbed Molly's tummy with his fingertips. "He's interested in her. I knew he would be."

Suspicion dawned bright and clear. "Garrett?" Molly said, sitting up straight and eyeing the self-satisfied smirk on her husband's roguish face.

"Yeah, babe?"

"What have you got up your sleeve?"

He looked at her with wide-eyed innocence. "Nothing, why?"

"You set this up, didn't you?" Molly accused.

"I don't know what you're talking—"

"Didn't you?" she prodded.

Molly knew him too well. Caught, Garrett had to come clean. "I didn't exactly set anything up. I just mentioned that this afternoon would be a good time for him to come talk to you about the dinner, that's all."

"Don't interfere."

"I'm not interfering," he denied.

Molly lifted auburn eyebrows. "Oh? What would you call it?"

"Cade's a damn nice guy," Garrett said, unable to meet her eyes. "They're both single. They're old buds. She'll have a few empty evenings to kill. I just thought that maybe they could have a few laughs while she's here."

Molly put her head back on his shoulder and was silent, thoughtful.

"Mol?" he said after a few moments.

"What?"

"What's going on in that pretty head of yours?" he asked.

"I'm thinking that pairing the two of them up isn't a bad idea," she said grudgingly. "But you forgot a couple of things."

"What's that?" Garrett asked with a frown.

"Cade Robichaux is very good-looking, but it's obvious that he must not be into long-term relationships. Your sister is very vulnerable right now. In fact, she's a prime candidate for a rebound relationship. I'd just hate to see her get hurt again."

The optimism in Garrett's eyes faded. "I hadn't thought about that. You're right."

Again, silence filled the already quiet room. "Mol?"

"Hmm?"

"Do you really think Cade is good-looking?"

Molly lifted her head and looked into her husband's eyes. "Oh, yeah," she said with a soft smile. "You've got a couple of handsome friends."

Garrett didn't miss the teasing twinkle in her eyes. He grinned. "Then maybe I'd better watch you around them."

"Nah," Molly said, sliding her fingers between the buttons of his shirt. "Who'd want an old pregnant woman like me?"

Garrett's eyes darkened as he lowered his head to her waiting lips. "I would."

Upstairs, in the unfamiliar bed, Shiloh tossed and turned. She thought about her conversation with Molly and wondered again about the sex of her child. She recalled the look on Jack's face as he'd held out the check to rid his life of her and his unwanted baby. And she thought of the moment she'd driven up and seen Cade on the steps with Laura.

She'd always heard children and dogs could be trusted when it came to judging people. If that was true, Cade must be a good man. Laura had clung to him, almost possessively, and she had been content to sit on his lap and listen to the adult conversation flow around her. In return, Cade had been patient, gentle, teasing. It was obvious that he doted on the lovely Laura Leigh.

Shiloh punched her pillow and turned it over to the cool side. It wasn't right—it wasn't even decent—for her to be so interested in a man she hadn't seen in almost twenty years, not when she'd thought herself so in love a month ago. It made her seem shallow, superficial. Superficial or not, she couldn't deny that she had been aware of Cade Robichaux in a very physical way.

Still, before she fell asleep she managed to convince herself that her unexpected, unwanted feelings for Cade were nothing but the remaining sparks of that long-ago summer crush.

Shiloh Rambler was the first image to enter Cade's head when he awoke on Sunday morning. He could still see the way her close-cropped hair framed her oval face and how shapely her legs were. The loose clothing she'd worn had teased him with the promise of firm curves. He tried to imagine what she would look like naked. The mental picture caused a tightening in his groin. The feeling was followed by a fleeting sense of guilt he did his best to squelch.

It was okay to be turned on by a beautiful woman. Especially when that woman was an old friend. Well, not exactly a friend, but there was a lot between them, like that time he was nineteen and had been accused of stealing a flatbed trailer full of hay.

When one of the other hands had pointed the finger at him, Jon Rambler had taken him aside and asked him where he'd been the night before. Cade had been embarrassed to admit that after being scorned by Pamela Hardy, the high school prom queen who'd led him on for months, he'd gotten nastily, sloppily drunk and, after puking up his guts, he'd spent the night down by the bayou in the back of his pickup truck.

The sorrow in Jon Rambler's eyes as Cade had volunteered the whole grim tale had been hard to take.

Not only had he felt like crud because he'd stooped to the very act he hated his father for, he'd disappointed the man who'd helped him the most. Even though Jon had said he believed him, there had been no one to vouch for his whereabouts. He'd been alone. When Garrett, who had overheard the confrontation between his dad and Cade, had told twelve-year-old Shiloh what was going on, she had burst into her father's office and offered him her story...verifying Cade's alibi.

From his spot across the room, Cade had stared at the shining top of her bowed head and listened in surprise as she had revealed to her father that she had a crush on Cade.

"I heard Cade say he was meeting Pamela down by the clearing near the bayou," she confessed, her voice quavering, her fingers knotted together. "I was... jealous, so I slipped out of bed and followed him."

Shocked by her confession, Cade glanced at Jon and saw the tightening of his lips. Cade knew from firsthand experience that her words were hurting her as much as his confession had devastated him just moments before.

There was compassion in his eyes as he looked in admiration at the young girl who was poised on the brink of womanhood and who, for an instant, raised tortured, tear-filled eyes to his.

"I wish I hadn't gone," she cried. "Pamela had been real flirty with Cade...getting...real close to him, acting like she liked him, but when he tried to kiss her, she just laughed. She laughed in his face!"

Her young voice broke. Pain pierced Cade's heart, but he wasn't certain if it was rooted in his own memory of Pamela's mocking laughter or the empathy and anguish emanating from Shiloh. Her tender twelve-year-old heart was hurting for him, and for that he felt humbled.

"Some of Pamela's friends stopped by, and she left with them. Cade stayed down at the bayou all night, Daddy, I promise he did!" She flicked an apologetic glance at Cade, as if to say she was sorry for telling on him, and rushed on. "He cussed and raved and then he got a bottle of liquor from behind the truck seat and he drank it all. He was real sick. I guess he finally went to sleep or passed out. I wanted to go to him and make sure he was okay, but I didn't think he'd want me to see him like that. I fell asleep, too, and when I woke up it was almost daytime and he was still there. There's no way he could have taken that hay."

Shiloh's corroboration of his story had kept the heat on, and the sheriff had finally discovered that the hay had been stolen by the same worker who'd put the finger on Cade. As a way of thanking her, he had gone to the florist and had a single pink rose sent to her. If he remembered correctly, Shiloh had been grounded for a week for slipping out of the house.

Cade wondered if she remembered the incident, or if she'd forgotten it along with her childhood crush. And he wondered if seeing him again had made her remember those long-ago feelings...or if they'd been rekindled.

What is this, Robichaux? Why the inordinate interest in Shiloh Rambler? There are two dozen women in town who would go out with you in a heartbeat, and they won't be leaving town in a few weeks.

True, but none of them interested him much. Though she had the gloss and polish of a sophisticated, successful woman, there was something about Shiloh that drew him. He wasn't sure if it was the pull of old memories or the hint of sorrow lurking in the shadowed depths of her blue eyes. Talks with Garrett indicated that all the fences had been mended between the Rambler kids and their dad, so the reason for her unhappiness must lie somewhere else. Maybe it was a man. Or maybe, like him, she was tired of being alone. Sick of being lonely.

A sudden thought flitted through his mind: maybe they could pass a few hours together while she was here. He nixed the idea almost as soon as it was born. Even though his social status had improved greatly, inside he was still the quiet kid from the wrong side of the tracks with all his old insecurities and inadequacies intact.

Still, as implausible as the idea seemed, the possibility of a date with Shiloh lingered. Just because she was the sister of a friend didn't mean she was off-limits, did it?

Don't be a fool. She's a Rambler.

But she wasn't a snob. He knew that for certain. And the seven years' difference in their ages wouldn't be a problem now. If she refused, it wouldn't be the end of the world. If she accepted, it would be just a date. She'd soon be going back to her restaurant business in Chattanooga, and they could both return to their lives...whatever excitement or boredom they might hold.

As he remembered that she owned her own restaurant, he got another idea. Why not see if *she* would cater his dinner instead of Molly? The house was at least a month from being ready for visitors, and Molly had been a bit reluctant to accept the undertaking so near her due date. If Shiloh was still going to be around, maybe she'd help them both out...and it was a way to get to spend time with her.

Cade's wry laughter rang out hollowly in the barrenness of the downstairs parlor as he punched out the Ramblers' number. He hadn't realized he was so desperate to spend time with a woman who really interested him. Damn if he wasn't sinking to new depths every day.

Molly answered the phone on the second ring.

"Molly. Cade. I had an idea I wanted to run past you," he said without preamble.

"And a good morning to you, too," Molly said cheerily.

"Sorry about that," he said with a sheepish grin. "Good morning. How are you?"

"Fine. And you?"

"Great."

"So what's this idea?" Molly asked.

Cade took a deep breath and plunged before he backed out. "I know you were concerned about the dinner being so close to your due date, so I started thinking that Shiloh might be interested in doing it— that is, if she's still going to be here."

There was a significant pause on the other end of the line. Molly was sharp; he wondered if she could read between the lines.

"That's a wonderful idea," she said at last. "Why don't you ask her?"

"Is she awake?"

"Ye-es." She dragged the word out into two syllables. "I'll get her."

In a matter of seconds Shiloh's soft Tennessee drawl was falling softly on his ears.

"Good morning."

"Hi. Sleep well?"

"Like a log," she said. He could hear the smile in her voice. "How about you?"

"Like a baby," he lied. Her low gasp brought a frown to his face. "Are you okay?"

"Fine. I almost spilled my coffee. What can I do for you?"

Her voice was crisp and businesslike, and Cade almost lost his nerve. Only the thought of her being in the neighborhood, so to speak, and the possibility of his not getting to spend any time with her bolstered his determination.

"I was wondering if you'd consider doing my business dinner for me in Molly's place." Before she could formulate her arguments, he continued. "Molly is afraid it will be too close to her delivery date, and you're certainly qualified."

He heard her sigh. "And I'm not exactly turning down social invitations by the drove, am I?"

"Hell, *chère,* you just got here," he teased, the seductive French endearment slipping out before he could stop it. "I thought I'd back you into a corner before your dance card got filled up."

"Fat chance."

"Of what?" he said in a low voice. "Your dance card getting filled up or me backing you into a corner?" The picture that leaped into his mind had nothing to do with dinners or dance cards.

Again he heard that sharply indrawn breath. "Either," she quipped back.

"Damn. So what do you say, *chère?*"

"Do I have to let you know right now?" she asked. "I just got up, and I'm not functional just yet."

He laughed and pushed the advantage of his surprise attack. "The sooner the better. If you say yes, I thought you could come over and we could start planning things."

"Today?" she queried.

"Why not?"

"It's Mother's Day. Garrett is taking me and Molly to lunch after church."

"Well, how about later this afternoon, after you get back?"

She was quiet a moment. "I guess that would be okay."

Cade laughed. "Does that mean you're going to cater the dinner?"

"It looks that way, doesn't it?" she said dryly. "Are you always so forceful?"

"I don't know," he admitted. "I believe in pressing any advantage I might have, and I don't like wasting valuable time. Procrastination isn't my style."

"I remember that," she said, and he could hear the thoughtful note in her voice. "You always did get things done."

"Then I haven't changed that much, have I?" he asked.

"You've changed."

He wanted to ask in what ways, wanted to keep her on the phone just so he could listen to her voice, but he figured he'd pushed all he could. "So have you," he told her, and heard the husky note that had crept into his own voice. "You've grown up into a very beautiful woman."

"Have I?"

Cade thought he detected a trace of wistfulness in the question. An unexpected twinge of pain tweaked his heart. "Fishing for compliments?" he taunted.

"Beast!" she said with a short laugh.

As he thought it might, his teasing had chased away whatever specter of sorrow haunted her. "See you this afternoon around three, three-thirty—okay?"

"Okay."

"Don't stand me up."

He heard her take a catchy breath. "I wouldn't dream of it."

Shiloh cradled the receiver and stood at the kitchen counter, Cade's throaty command still ringing in her ears, a bemused expression on her face.

"Are you going to do it?"

At the sound of Molly's voice, she turned. Her brother and sister-in-law were regarding her, their eyes full of questions. She cleared her throat and shrugged. "Why not? I'm going to be here for almost a month, and it isn't as if I'm busy or anything. Once we get the menu worked out, all it'll take is a day for shopping and a couple of days' preparation." Then, as if she'd just thought of it, she asked, "You don't mind, do you, Molly?"

Molly shook her gleaming head. "Honey, you're doing me a favor. Can you imagine what these ankles will look like in another month?"

A wave of relief washed through Shiloh. "He wants me to come over this afternoon when we get back from lunch so we can talk things over."

Garrett and Molly looked at each other. Molly's face wore an expression Shiloh couldn't define, and Garrett lifted his dark eyebrows. Molly murmured something from the corner of her mouth. All Shiloh got was "waste much time." Garrett's unintelligible response sounded like "My hero."

"What?" Shiloh asked, her puzzled gaze moving from one to the other.

Molly gave Garrett a hush-your-mouth look and pinned Shiloh with a bright smile. "I said, look at the time. More coffee?"

"Please," Shiloh said, but she wasn't diverted. "Is anything wrong?"

"Not a thing, babe," Garrett assured her with a smug grin. "Everything's as right as rain."

Chapter Four

Before Shiloh's arrival Cade changed clothes twice, finally settling on a knit pullover, faded jeans and scuffed boots—so she wouldn't think he was trying to make an impression. He was pacing the floor of the front parlor when he heard Shiloh's car pull into the gravel driveway. He wasn't aware that a sigh of relief escaped from him. He watched her get out of the car and look around at the exterior renovations that were under way. The light of genuine interest gleamed in her eyes.

Cade was looking at *her* with a fair amount of genuine interest. She was wearing a candy-pink-and-white-striped sundress. The fitted bodice had wide shoulder straps and cupped the fullness of her breasts like a lover's hand, while the short, pencil-slim skirt molded her firm derriere and thighs with a breath-stopping accuracy. White pumps emphasized the shapeliness of her calves and the trimness of her ankles.

Swearing in true masculine appreciation, Cade stepped through the leaded-glass door, doing his best to suppress a sappy grin.

"Hi," he said, crossing the wooden expanse of the porch.

Shiloh was fingering a cluster of rambling roses that exactly matched the pink of her dress. Both her pink-tinted lips and her eyes smiled. "Hi."

"You're on time." As soon as the words left his lips Cade felt like a fool. There was something about the grown-up Shiloh Rambler that made him feel like a callow sixteen-year-old again.

"Well, you sounded as if you were in a hurry to get things done," she reminded him, clutching her white straw purse close.

He grinned down at her. "Touché." He made a sweeping gesture. "Would you like the nickel tour before we get started?"

"If you're sure you can spare the time." Her tone was dead serious, but mischief danced in her eyes.

He headed down the steps and joined her on the brick walkway. "I think we have a few minutes," he responded in the same vein.

"Then I'd love to look around."

"Let's start outside, then—" he glanced at her feet "—if you can handle the terrain in those high heels."

"Surely you've learned from Sunny that little girls are born knowing how to handle high heels," she teased.

A cloud passed over Cade's features. "I've missed a lot of things about little girls, since I wasn't able to be around Sunny every day."

Rather than pursue the topic, Shiloh took his arm. "Well, I can't be here every day, either, but I don't want to miss a thing."

It crossed his mind that it would be nice to have Shiloh there every day, though he dismissed the fleeting thought as ludicrous. It had been a long time since he'd had a meaningful relationship with a woman, and apparently he was confusing his rampaging hormones and the fact that Shiloh Rambler was the stuff dreams were made of with more lasting emotions. Hell, for all that they'd been acquaintances for years, the truth was that he hardly knew the woman. Even so, it was impossible to imagine that waking up next to her every morning would be a hardship.

She pointed to a trio of brick buildings standing well away from the house. "Are those slave quarters?"

Cade cleared his throat of the huskiness fostered by his daydream. "Yeah. Those three are all that are left. I converted one into an office. Would you like to see it?"

"I'd love to."

The humming of a window air conditioner hinted of the coolness they found inside the small building. Shiloh looked around her with unconcealed interest. The brick walls had been sandblasted and left natural. Diplomas and awards adorned one wall and a pair of Frank McCarthy prints—both noble-looking Native Americans, both signed by the artist and bearing identical numbers—hung in a place of prominence over the fireplace. A television and VCR stood against a far wall and a stack of video game cartridges sat nearby. An oak rolltop desk and matching filing cabinets completed the masculine decor. A computer sat on the desk, which looked as if the legs had been cut off to make it the right working height. The room was done in cream, sable brown and forest green.

"It's very nice," she said, finished with her perusal. "I didn't know you liked Western art."

"I didn't, either, until a few years ago. I started looking for something to invest in that I could enjoy. A friend took me to an art dealer in New Orleans, and I was hooked. I have others in the house. They all just—" he shrugged, unable to express his feelings "—speak to me in some way."

"Maybe it's because the Native Americans are such a wonderful part of our heritage."

"Maybe."

She picked up one of the video game boxes that bore the name of a Civil War battle and the slogan Your Chance To Rewrite History. "What made you start creating video games?"

"At first it was just a way to earn extra money at something I was good at," he said without hesitation. "But it was my love of history—especially the Civil War—that prompted me to do this newest series."

"How do they work?"

"You don't want to hear about that." Cade had never been one to brag about his work and, despite the fact that her interest seemed genuine, he liked talking about it with Shiloh even less than most people. He didn't want her to think he was tooting his own horn.

"If I didn't want to know, I wouldn't have asked."

Giving a resigned shrug, he turned on the television and VCR and inserted the game. In a matter of seconds a computer-generated picture of the commanding officers for this particular battle filled the screen, along with the command for each player to choose which person he wanted to be.

"In a nutshell, the games pit two or more players—who take the roles of the Northern and Southern generals—against each other." He hit a couple of buttons, and a layout of the battlefield appeared. "They have a playing field that simulates as closely as possible the place of the battle, the terrain, the maps—basically, they get the same information and same number of troops the real generals had. Each player uses that information and makes his battle decisions based on that knowledge." He grinned lopsidedly. "It gives us Rebs a chance to change the outcome."

"Your chance to rewrite history," she said, reading the promotional gimmick from the box.

"Exactly."

"It sounds as if it would take someone very smart to figure it all out."

"Or very hungry." Abruptly he turned away to stare out the window. Tension held his back straight and stiff.

Shiloh knew he was referring to his childhood. What there had been of it. "Have you created Shiloh yet?" she asked, hoping to break the spell of melancholy gripping him.

He turned, a question in his eyes. "Pardon?"

"Have you recreated the Battle of Shiloh?"

The tautness eased from his body, but a frown still knitted his forehead. "It comes out in time for Christmas."

"Good timing."

"Yeah. Speaking of timing, this may not be the best, but I always wanted to ask how you got named after one of the bloodiest battles of history."

"That's why."

"I beg your pardon?"

"I'm told my parents fought like cats and dogs during their first marriage to each other, and it got worse while Mama was pregnant with me. I was late coming, and Daddy was supposed to make a business trip. Finally he couldn't wait any longer. He left one morning, and Mama had me that evening. To this day he swears she did it on purpose."

Shiloh smiled. "He's probably right. As for my name, she claims to have liked it, the battle *was* fought in Tennessee and, since she and Daddy fought so much during the pregnancy, she thought the name was perfect, all of which translates to one thing. She figured it would make him furious, and it did. They divorced before I was a year old. But not because of that," she added hastily.

"But they're happy now?"

"To quote Molly, they're as happy as two fat hogs in the sunshine."

Cade laughed. "So what kind of middle name do you put with a battle?"

Her lips curved into an enticing smile. "Camille. Pure Southern."

"Shiloh Camille," he said in a soft, thoughtful voice that sent a shiver tripping down her spine. "Strong and soft. Just the way you are."

She was surprised by his observation. Her awareness of him as a virile, handsome man surged from the place she'd tried so hard to banish it. "How do you know what I'm like?" she asked in a voice that held only the barest bit of breathlessness.

"I watched you grow up, remember? Our outward trappings may change, and hopefully we grow and mature, but I'm convinced that unless—or until—

something catastrophic happens, most of us don't change a whole lot deep down inside where it counts."

"That's pretty profound."

He looked embarrassed. "Or stupid. Let's go inside."

He curled his strong fingers around her arm and they made the trek back to the house. Inside, he took her on a room-to-room tour, explaining what was being done, moaning about the myriad problems he'd run into and telling her about a couple of decorating ideas he had.

They were in the room where he slept, which was currently furnished only with a tester bed and highboy, when Shiloh spotted several photographs of a young man and a teenage girl.

"Are those your children?"

"Yeah."

She crossed to the chest and picked up the picture of his daughter. Sparkling brown eyes smiled out from beneath a mop of fashionable spiral curls that tumbled onto her forehead and brushed her shoulders. It was hard to imagine Cade having children, but the young woman smiling back at her was undeniably his. "She's beautiful. She looks a lot like you."

"She does?"

Cade moved behind her and regarded the photo of his daughter over her shoulder. Again that mind-boggling consciousness flared, making it next to impossible to keep her thoughts focused on the image before her. She drew a steadying breath; the scent of his cologne sent her senses adrift on a sea of longing so intense it frightened and appalled her. It seemed like forever since she'd nuzzled a man's neck and inhaled those sensuous masculine aromas.

Determined to squash the feelings if it killed her, she pointed to Sunny's chin. "Do you see that? If that isn't a Cade Robichaux chin I've never seen one." She shook her head. "Lord, I can't believe you have nearly grown kids."

"Me, either. Sunny just has two more years of high school, and Jared will be a college sophomore next year. I'm just beginning to realize how much I've missed by not being with them every day." There was a definite air of wistfulness in his voice. "We aren't as close as I'd like."

"That's common even with families who do live together," she told him, wanting to soothe the hurt she sensed dwelled deep inside him. "I think they call it a generation gap."

He nodded. "I suppose you're right, but I don't like it. There are a lot of things I'm finding I'm not crazy about. Like being alone." His smile lacked any semblance of humor. "Until lately, I never thought much about growing old, and now when I do think about it, it scares the hell out of me. I think it's the idea of growing old alone that's so hard to take."

Shiloh nodded. "I can relate to that."

"No special man in your life?"

It was hard to meet the directness of his gaze. How could she tell him that her own dream of finding someone to grow old with had died with Jack Delaney's rejection? "No," she said. "No special man." The curtness of her tone prohibited further questioning.

Anxious to change the subject, she put down Sunny's picture and reached for Jared's. "Oh, Cade, he's so handsome. You know, he looks like you, too. They both have eyes shaped just like yours."

Without weighing the consequences of her actions, she glanced up at him over her shoulder and bestowed one of her wrinkle-nose smiles on him. "Bedroom eyes."

In the instant before she looked away, she saw that Cade's bedroom eyes had darkened with an emotion that sent her pulse racing.

"If you think both my kids are so good-looking and that they look like me, does that mean you think I'm good-looking?" he asked in a husky voice that compelled her to turn and confront not only him but the emotions building between them.

Shiloh knew she was digging herself in deeper, but she couldn't help herself. There was a boldness in her manner as she faced him that was at odds with the trembling in her legs. "You don't need me to tell you you're handsome."

He started to reach out and touch her, but she pivoted back around and set Jared's picture on top of the bureau, shattering the tense moment. When she turned back toward Cade, the famous Rambler poker face was firmly in place. The disappointment in his eyes was tempered with resignation.

She glanced around the room. "It's going to be fantastic. I'd love to see it when it's finished."

"Don't worry, *chère,* you will."

Shiloh's heart leaped at the unexpected endearment and the promise of the two simple words.

"How about a glass of iced tea?" he asked abruptly.

"Sounds great."

Cade led her into the kitchen and seated her at the walnut draw-leaf table. Natural brick walls and gleaming cypress floors were brightened by white shutters and appliances. A plethora of gleaming an-

tique copper utensils in every shape and size sat on or
were hung in strategic places throughout the room.
Green plants lent additional color and a feeling of
outdoors to the rustic room.

"You need a green-and-white rag rug under the table," she commented, thinking out loud.

Cade, who was pouring the tea, turned and looked
at the table thoughtfully. "That would be nice. Any
other ideas?"

She laughed. "If it was my house, I'd have loads of
ideas!"

He set the glasses down and took a seat across from
her. "I'd like to hear your suggestions."

"Oh, Cade, I'm a woman. You're a man."

"I noticed that," he said, undermining her defenses with ridiculous ease.

Shiloh lifted her glass of tea to hide the rush of hot
color that rose in her cheeks. "I mean, we're bound to
have different likes and dislikes."

"You like what I've done so far, so we can't be that
far off track," he pointed out. "Look, I'm flying by
the seat of my pants here. I don't know a damn thing
about decorating. I just do what I think I'd like."

"Well, the outcome looks wonderful."

He lifted his broad shoulders. "See? We're com-
patible. Shoot. What would you do with that bedroom upstairs that has all the windows?"

"That's easy. I saw a comforter I was crazy about
the other day. It had purple violets on a white background. I'd paint the floor forest green, the walls
white, put billowing white curtains at the windows and
use white wicker and green plants throughout the
room."

"It sounds great. Light and airy...like spring-time."

"You don't think it would be too feminine?"

He shrugged. "I don't have to sleep there. Even if I did, I think the overall feel of the house is more important than whether I sleep in a room with flowers."

"You're a rare man," Shiloh said thoughtfully.

"Yeah. Tell that to my ex."

The comment roused Shiloh's curiosity. She couldn't help asking, "What about your ex?"

"What happened to my marriage, you mean?"

"I'd like to know, if you don't mind telling me."

"Why should I mind? It was common enough knowledge when she left me. I think she told the whole of Thibodaux. Those she didn't tell, her mama did."

"You had an affair?" she blurted in surprise, her face flaming as she said it.

"No. She claimed I didn't love her when we got married."

"Did you?"

"I thought I did. Hell, that's not true," he said with a shake of his head. Brutal honesty reposed in his eyes. "The truth is that I'd never thought much about love—real love. Mary Rose was a decent girl, and the sex was good. I guess I thought that what I felt was love and that somewhere down the line we'd get married and have our two-point-five kids."

He gave another negative shake of his dark head. "It didn't work that way. She came to me one day and said she was pregnant, so we had to get married. No, I take that back. She was pregnant, but I guess I didn't *have* to marry her." He laughed shortly. "When she told me about the baby, the thought of having two more people dependent on me scared me to death, but

I knew that I was as much to blame as she was, and I damn sure wasn't gonna be like my daddy and run out on my obligations. In that respect, I did want to marry her."

He drew in a deep breath. "So we got married, and by the time Sunny came along Mary Rose said she was sick of coming in a bad second to my work. She used to tell me that I was married to my jobs and that she'd rather be competing with a woman."

"Was she right?"

A look of sorrow shadowed his eyes. "Yeah, *chère,* she was," he admitted without hesitation. "I was working for General Dynamics in Fort Worth and working as much overtime as they'd give me. Then by some sort of fluke I started creating games for a video company, and then, about four years ago, this deal came up with Nintendo. The rest, as they say, is history."

"You're a success."

"Oh, yeah, I'm a helluva success. I worked hard and made damn sure my family was provided for—only thing is, that I was so busy securing their future, I lost them somewhere along the way."

Shiloh couldn't bear the bitterness in his eyes. He'd done what he thought was right, which was all anyone could be expected to do. On the other hand, she understood Mary Rose's feelings; even so, the woman must have been a fool to let a man like this slip through her fingers. She certainly wouldn't. The errant realization sent her surging to her feet. "How about some more tea?"

"I'll get it."

She put a restraining hand on his shoulder and felt the warmth of his flesh through the knit fabric of his shirt. "No. Sit. It feels strange having a man wait on me. I guess I'm a little old-fashioned in some respects."

"You're a rare woman, Shiloh Rambler," he said, tossing back her earlier comment. His eyes feasted on her face as she poured the tea.

"Hardly."

"You're also a very interesting, beautiful woman, and I'd like to take you to dinner while you're here."

Despite the interest he'd shown, the invitation took her by surprise. Holding a sprig of mint in her hand, she turned to face him. The plea in his eyes wreaked havoc with her resolve. She shook her head, and her dangling earrings brushed her cheeks. "I can't."

She saw the muscle in his cheek tighten. Intuition told her that he'd misunderstood her reasonig again.

"Won't, you mean. Why, Shiloh? Too many memories of the old Cade Robichaux and where he came from?"

"Of course not!" Her denial was emphatic. She wanted to tell him that she was afraid to go out with him, afraid that the feelings his nearness ignited would only grow, a situation she couldn't allow because she was pregnant with another man's child.

"I'm a lot of things, but I'm not a snob." She leaned her hip against the cabinet in utter weariness and forced her eyes to his. "The truth is, I'm just coming out of a relationship, and I don't think I'm ready to jump into another."

"I'm not asking for a relationship. Just dinner."

"I don't think so," she said again, "but thank you."

Cade nodded. "He broke things off, didn't he?"

She glanced at him, surprise in her blue eyes. "Does it matter who broke things off?"

"Of course it does. If you gave him the brush, you wouldn't hesitate to accept a date. But if he broke off with you, then you're having trouble with your pride, as well as nursing a broken heart—which you seem to be doing."

Shiloh's teeth clamped onto her bottom lip and she battled the urge to cry—or scream. He was right, of course...about everything. She gave a helpless shrug. "You're right. Jack called it off."

"And is your heart broken?" Cade asked in a gentle voice.

A wry smile twisted her lips as she turned away. "Let's say it took a pretty good beating."

"Ten to one that in a few months' time you'll realize that your ego was bruised worse than your heart."

"I hope so." She dropped the sprig of mint into the glass and picked it up.

"Shiloh?"

She looked up.

"Whoever he is, he's a fool."

"No," she countered with a shake of her head. "I was the fool." She'd taken no more than two steps toward him when the room began to whirl. She stopped, a queasy expression on her face.

Cade leaped to his feet and crossed the small space separating them in three long strides. "What's the matter?"

She felt his arm go around her shoulder and, fighting another wave of light-headedness, she leaned into his strength and warmth as naturally as water runs downhill. He lifted her chin with his forefinger.

"What's wrong?"

She tried to smile through the darkness that still beckoned, but it was a miserable failure. "I don't know," she said, but she did know. Jack's baby was reminding her that she had no business feeling the things this man made her feel. "I just felt dizzy all of a sudden."

"Are you all right now?"

"I'm fine," she lied. Forcing the remnants of dizziness aside, she pushed herself free of the security of Cade's arms. "Did I spill any tea on you?"

"No." He took the glass from her and slid an arm around her waist. "Come on. Sit down."

Grateful, Shiloh complied. He handed her the glass and she took a sip of her own drink. The lightheadedness was passing as quickly as it had come on.

Wearing a worried frown, Cade sat across from her. "How're you feeling?"

"Better," she said with a halfhearted smile. "Fine, really."

"Liar."

"Really," she insisted, resting her elbows on the table. Dropping her head, she began to massage her temples with her fingertips.

He nodded. "If you're up to the drive, why don't you go on home and get some rest."

She glanced up. "I thought you wanted to discuss the menu for the dinner."

"Does this mean you're definitely going to do it?"

"I thought we'd already established that."

One corner of his mouth lifted in a derisive smile. "That was before I started trying to hit on you. I figured there was a strong possibility you might have changed your mind."

Her steady blue gaze met his. "I haven't."

"Good. If you start feeling better, you can work up two or three menus. We'll talk about them tomorrow. Fair enough?"

"Fair enough."

She was rising to go when the back door opened and Jared, whom she recognized from his picture, and a young woman came bursting through, chattering ninety to nothing. Both were stylishly and expensively dressed in shorts, shirts and hundred-dollar tennis shoes.

When Jared saw Shiloh sitting at the table he pulled up short. Even in its brevity, the quick once-over he gave her missed nothing. Cade, the product of another generation, rose when the girl entered the room. "Hello, son," he said politely. "Who's your friend?"

"Katy Mercer. Who's yours?" There was a hint of sarcasm in Jared's voice. Katy stood back in silence, wanting no part of the tension building between the two men.

Seeing the muscle in Cade's jaw tighten with sudden anger, which he managed to hold in check, Shiloh smiled and held out her hand.

"Hello, Jared. I'm Shiloh Rambler. Your dad and I used to know each other a long time ago."

"Yeah?" His manners surfaced, and Jared crossed the few feet separating them and took her hand, albeit reluctantly. He didn't return her smile.

"I used to work for her father," Cade said.

Jared couldn't have cared less. "No kidding?"

Again Shiloh saw Cade rein in his anger. "Would you two like a glass of iced tea?" he asked, attempting to be sociable.

"Don't have time," Jared said. "Bobby's having a big cookout, and everyone has to chip in for the food. I'm broke."

Cade's gaze bored into his son's. "So you need money again?"

Shiloh thought Jared's belligerence faded a little beneath his father's blatant disgust. "Yeah. Twenty bucks should do it."

Cade reached into his back pocket and pulled out his wallet. He took out a twenty and handed it to his son. "Did you go see about that summer job I told you about?"

Jared's face grew beet red. "Not yet."

"When do you plan to go?"

"Tomorrow," Jared said, already heading for the door. "I promise." He opened the door to leave. Katy followed in silence.

"Jared."

He turned. It was obvious that he didn't want to hear anything else Cade might have to say on the subject. "Sir?"

"You will go see about it tomorrow." Though he didn't say it, the implication was clear: if Jared didn't try to get the job, he wouldn't be getting any more money from Cade. Though she knew Jared must be embarrassed at having her and Katy witness the skirmish between him and his dad, Shiloh couldn't blame Cade for his stand.

"Yes, sir."

The door closed behind them, almost obliterating Katy's "Nice to meet you both."

Cade sat down heavily. "I'm sorry he was so rude."

"He wasn't rude. Just in a hurry."

"Like hell. He was rude."

"Is he usually jealous when you have a woman over?" Shiloh asked.

Cade's disturbed gaze met hers. "He isn't crazy about it. I can't imagine why. He must know I date, and Mary Rose has been married forever. He didn't have a problem accepting Michael."

"He was younger and more accepting then. Kids tend to be selfish with parents. Maybe he's afraid he'll lose you if you get married again."

"Yeah, sure," Cade scoffed. "I mean, it isn't like we're bosom buddies or anything."

"And that bothers you, doesn't it?" she asked, her voice rich with empathy.

His devil-ridden eyes met hers. He nodded. "It does, *chère,* and I'm damned if I know what to do about it. I can't turn back the clock and make my marriage work. I can't replace all the years the kids and I missed together. The hell of it is that I was doing what I thought was right, and somehow none of it seems fair."

It wasn't fair, she thought an hour later as she lay in her bed and mulled over the afternoon she'd spent with Cade. It wasn't fair that her dizziness should cut her afternoon short or that, once she'd gotten home, her back had started aching so fiercely that she'd had to come up to bed. It wasn't fair that Cade should be able to disarm her with that slow, sexy smile of his or that she couldn't act on the feelings he aroused inside her.

What did he arouse? Awareness. Sexual awareness. That much was undeniable. That this awareness bothered her was also undeniable. Would she feel this sensual longing for Cade, or any other man, if she truly loved Jack? Or was Cade's prediction that her pride was hurt closer to target? Was her bruised ego feeding off the attention of another man—Cade—in an effort to bolster her flagging self-esteem? *Was* it her pride and not her heart that was smarting from Jack's refusal to commit?

Shiloh eased to her side and punched her pillow with a fist. She was beginning to fear that the answer to those questions was yes, beginning to fear that what she'd felt for Jack wasn't real love, beginning to think she'd been so caught up in Jack's skillful courting, so flattered by the attention he'd paid her that she'd mistaken infatuation for the real thing. Unfortunately, that possibility didn't ease her guilt over the feelings ignited by Cade's nearness. On the contrary, it made her wonder—and fear—that she might be guilty of doing the same thing again.

Depression engulfed her. What if these feelings weren't real, either? What if she was just so desperate to find love that she would fall for any line handed to her? She was vulnerable right now, there was no doubt about that. And, if it wasn't for the baby growing inside her, it would be easy to allow herself to get involved with Cade in a rebound situation.

She sighed in frustration. Despite her ambivalence—whether to her aching heart or her bruised ego—Cade's attentions were a soothing balm. She wished the nagging recurring backaches were so easily remedied.

Chapter Five

The following afternoon, Monday, Shiloh wandered through a new antique store just outside Raceland, pondering the ease with which Cade had talked her into going shopping with him and knowing that it boiled down to pure weakness on her part. They had started out looking for glassware and china, which they had purchased in New Orleans three hours and four stores ago. But they were still shopping...just in case they ran into something that was dying to go home with him, Cade said.

Recalling the comment, her sharp gaze swept from right to left, her eyes skimming the merchandise displayed to its best advantage. Though she wasn't looking for anything in particular, she knew she'd know it when, or if, she saw it.

She couldn't deny that it had been a fun day, though she'd learned that Cade Robichaux turned feminine heads wherever they went. They'd left soon after breakfast and driven to the French Quarter where Cade complimented and flirted and haggled over prices in a way that indicated that he'd done it many times before.

After buying two silver candlesticks, twelve place settings of Spode china and two dozen Waterford glasses at very reasonable prices, they'd called it a day. After a delicious lunch, which was now not agreeing with her very well, they'd started home, a prolonged trip since he insisted on stopping at every antique store along the way. She was tired, but it was a pleasant weariness; her backache of the day before was a distant memory. If only the nausea and slight stomach cramps that had nagged at her ever since she'd eaten lunch would go away, she'd be fine. Whatever happened to *morning* sickness? she wondered crossly.

"Hey, *chère,* how do you like this?" From a spot several yards away, Cade pointed to a globe lamp with flowers painted on the base.

Grimacing at a sudden cramp, she shook her head.

"That bad, huh?" he said with a grin.

She crossed the space separating them in what felt like slow motion. "Not bad, but I don't like that green. Too drab."

"Well, the face you made looked like you'd just taken a bite of a green persimmon."

So much for trying to hide how she was feeling. She tried to smile. "I'm sorry, but I've been feeling a little sick ever since lunch. Do you mind if we go home now?"

Cade's eyes filled with immediate concern, but his tone was teasing, light. "You fancy French chefs aren't used to all those hot, spicy seasonings in our Cajun food, are you?" he said.

"No, we're not."

He stepped closer and, placing a knuckle beneath her chin, tilted her face up for closer inspection. "Why didn't you say something sooner?"

"I didn't want to ruin the day," she confessed, the truth of the statement reflected in her eyes. "I was having too much fun."

"Were you?"

Shiloh thought he looked inordinately pleased at the possibility of her enjoying the time they'd spent together. Only an honest answer would do. "Yes."

"I'm glad." He smiled and took her arm. "Come on, *chère,* let's get you home."

She nodded, but felt a sense of sadness that the pleasant day had to end. There had been nothing exciting about it, but she'd enjoyed it every bit as much as she'd enjoyed the fabulous evenings she'd spent with Jack . . . which just went to prove that it was the companion, not the activity, that determined a good time.

Ensconced in Cade's Bronco, Shiloh sank back against the seat, closed her eyes and let her mind drift as the cooling breath of the air-conditioning wafted over her. Just as she succumbed to a brief and restless sleep, she thought how nice it would be to have a husband like Cade, one who didn't mind going shopping with a woman for such things as china and knick-knacks.

Thursday morning found her back at Magnolia Manor, three very different menus in hand. Though her nausea had thus far hit at different times with no apparent rhyme or reason, it had chosen that morning to settle into its rightful spot—and with a vengeance. By the time she reached Magnolia Manor she'd already been sick twice. She didn't feel like pretending that she was fine, but unless she wanted to tell everyone the truth, she had no choice.

The two days since she'd seen Cade had dragged interminably. The truth was, she missed seeing him. He had called to check on how she was feeling on Monday evening, but she'd already gone to bed. The next morning Molly relayed the message that she was to give Cade a call when she had the menus worked out. Wanting to see him, needing the gentle strength that was such a part of him and hating herself for her weakness, she had held off until Wednesday evening, when she'd broken down and called to ask if she could bring the menus over.

He'd suggested breakfast at his place Thursday morning; she'd declined, saying she'd stop by around nine-thirty. And here she was, pretending to sip a cup of coffee, listening to what he was asking her with half an ear and wishing it was after lunch so that the nausea churning inside her would have passed.

"So we're decided on the French onion soup, a salad of mushrooms *en champagne,* and veal with asparagus tips for the entrée," he said, ticking off items on his list.

Without answering, Shiloh raised the coffee to her lips, got a whiff of it, set it back down and swallowed hard. How long did the sickness—morning or otherwise—last, anyway? she wondered, closing her eyes and pushing the cup aside.

"What do you think for dessert?"

"I beg your pardon?" she asked, glancing over at him.

"The dessert?"

Shiloh lifted trembling fingers to her lips. "I thought you wanted the strawberries Romanoff."

"Oh, yeah. I forgot." He scribbled it down. "Did you see the wallpaper samples I picked up for the dining room?"

Instead of answering, Shiloh leaped up, tipping her chair in her haste, and ran through the house to the half bath Cade had installed beneath the stairs. She heard him calling, heard the scrape of his chair, but she couldn't answer, couldn't stop. She barely got the door shut behind her and dropped to her knees before she was violently sick.

Minutes later she grabbed hold of the pedestal sink and pulled herself to her feet. The mirror above the sink reflected back a pale, unappealing face. The dark circles beneath her eyes had nothing to do with the tear-streaked mascara lining her cheeks. She looked terrible—a wreck—and she had to go out there and face Cade. She rinsed out her mouth and splashed cold water on her hot face. Then, taking a wad of tissues from the box sitting on the back of the commode, she wiped at the mascara smeared around her eyes. Clutching the tissues, she squared her shoulders and, searching desperately for a lie that he might buy, she opened the door.

Seeing Shiloh jump up from the table and run from the room took Cade by surprise. He didn't know what to think except that obviously something was wrong. It was only as he stood outside the bathroom door and listened to the sounds of her retching that he began to suspect what that something was. The possibility was mind-boggling. Heart-wrenching. Stunned, not wanting to believe what his gut instinct was telling him, he went to a chair situated across the wide hallway and buried his head in his hands.

Shiloh was pregnant. So much for the idea of waking up in bed beside her. The unexpected depth of his pain gave him pause. Had he underestimated his feelings for her? Oh, he was willing to admit that she had garnered more than a fair share of his daydreams and nighttime fantasies this past week, but he'd never imagined that he was so entranced with her that the thought of her being pregnant by another man would knock the props out from under him this way. And yet, it wasn't the knowledge of the baby that was the source of his pain. It was knowing that Shiloh Rambler wasn't the kind to give either her heart or her body casually. She must have loved the guy a hell of a lot. No doubt she still loved him.

He gave a despairing sigh. No wonder she refused to go out with him. No wonder she was upset over the jerk breaking off with her. A sudden thought surfaced. Did this Jack guy know about the baby? And if he did, how could he be such a bastard and turn his back not only on his child, but its mother?

The doorknob rattled and Cade looked up, unaware that concern and anguish rested in his eyes, unaware that he looked older than he had mere minutes before, unaware of anything but the tortured rhythm of his heartbeats and the wary fear in Shiloh's eyes. She looked as terrible as he felt. Pale, ashen, really. As she stood there just looking at him, tears filled her eyes, but she didn't allow them to fall.

"I'm pregnant," she said, twisting her hands together.

"I know." His voice was low and controlled, and he could see that his admission surprised her.

"I want you to know that I'm not sad over Jack. I'm sad because...because..." Her voice trailed away and she shrugged. She couldn't tell him she was mourning a loss she was only just beginning to understand. "How did you know?"

"I never considered the possibility until just now, but then I remembered Mary Rose's symptoms, and I started putting it all together—the upset stomach, the dizziness."

Swiping at the threatening tears with the wad of tissues in her hand, she shook her head. "I should have known he wasn't real, that none of it was real!" she cried in anger and humiliation. "I can't believe I was so stupid!"

Unable to bear her self-castigation, Cade rose and went to her. Without considering the wisdom of his actions, wanting only to offer her what comfort he could, he pulled her into his arms. "Loving someone is never stupid," he told her. "Even when we fall for the wrong people. It shows that our hearts can be touched."

She looked up at him, and he could see that she wanted to believe him. Then, like a child, she laid her head back down against him and slid her arms around his waist. Cade held her and rubbed her back in an effort to ease her sorrow.

After a while he became less aware of her misery and more aware of the curvy body pressed so close to his. Her smallness made him feel big and clumsy. It also made him feel protective and somehow very much a man. He could feel the softness of her breasts, the warmth of her thighs, the way she held him . . . almost possessively.

Wishful thinking, Robichaux. The lady is still in love with the father of her child. He sighed.

Something of his frustration or the sound of his dismay must have transmitted itself to her. She gave an embarrassed, shaky laugh and stepped out of his embrace. "I'm sorry," she said. "I didn't mean to go to pieces that way."

"No problem." He offered no words of consolation; he didn't have any. "Does he know about the baby?"

"Yes." The word was a tortured whisper.

"What did he say when you told him?"

Shiloh clamped her teeth over her bottom lip to still its trembling. When she spoke her voice shook with more anger than pain. "He tried to give me a check for an abortion so I could get on with my life."

Shiloh cringed at the soft obscenity that flew unchecked from Cade's mouth. He plowed his hand through his hair, crossed to the fireplace and stalked back. "Does your family know?"

She shook her head.

"Don't you think you should tell them?"

"I will. I just . . . I'm afraid they'll be . . . disappointed."

He reached out and trailed a finger over the sweet-curving line of her jaw. "Oh, *chère*," he said softly. "Haven't you realized yet that that's what people do best—disappoint each other?"

"But Garrett has always been the hell-raiser. I've always been the perfect child, the one you could count on to do what's right."

"Then you were due a mistake, weren't you?"

"Maybe," she acknowledged, crossing her arms over her breasts and shaking her head. "I just don't understand how I could have been so wrong about Jack."

"My mother used to say that everything happens for a reason, and the older I get, the more I tend to believe her."

"What possible good could come out of this?" she asked. "Everyone will find out soon, and they'll think I'm cheap and easy."

"This is the nineties, *chère*. Women have babies out of wedlock every day. No one thinks much of it anymore."

"Maybe so, but I'm afaid I won't be able to handle it when they whisper about me behind my back."

Again, Cade had no solace to offer her. Coming to grips with the situation was something she'd have to do on her own. "Some of them probably will talk," he agreed. "Have you seen a doctor?"

"No." She could see her confession annoyed him. "Why not?"

"I guess I was trying to forget about it," she said.

"Damn it, Shiloh! You need to see a doctor. That baby isn't going to go away if you just ignore it, you know. You both need proper care—vitamins, that kind of stuff."

"I know, I know," she said a trifle angrily. "I'll go when I get back home."

"Home, as in Chattanooga? No way. That's three weeks away. You'll go as soon as I can make an appointment for you." He was already headed for the telephone.

"I don't know any good doctors here!" she cried, following him to the phone.

"I do. Ted Devane in Thibodaux. He's supposed to be one of the best."

As he picked up the receiver she grabbed his arm. "Did anyone ever tell you you were bossy? That you have the finesse of a steamroller?"

His slow smile made her heart race. "A time or two."

"I can't let you just take over this way," she told him firmly. "It isn't your place."

Cade removed her hand gently but with equal firmness. "The way I see it, *chère,* you don't have much to say about it."

He must have had some sort of pull, because Ted Devane was able to "work her in" the following afternoon. She left Magnolia Manor thirty minutes later, feeling as if she'd just missed out on something valuable. At the same time, she felt acute relief that her secret was out. Now all she had to do was tell Garrett and Molly... and of course her parents.

At his insistence, Cade picked Shiloh up the following afternoon and drove her into Thibodaux for her appointment. They spent the time during the drive talking about his kids and his fragile relationship with them.

"Sunny reminds me a lot of you," he told her. "And I guess I remind myself of your dad."

"Really? How?"

"When you were a kid I had the feeling you worshiped the ground Jon Rambler walked on."

"I did. And he didn't know I was alive."

"That's not true. I'd see him watch you do something and there would be this look of pride on his face, but all he'd do was give you an awkward pat on the shoulder or tell you you'd done well. I don't think he knew how to break down the wall between you."

"A hug would have helped," Shiloh said. "Or just thirty minutes of his precious time."

"I know, but looking at it from Jon's point of view, I can tell you that it's harder than you think—especially when you've missed out on so much because of time and distance. It's hard to know what to say, what even interests a child, when you don't have that daily interaction."

"He should have tried harder. You should try harder."

"Maybe you're right. Sometimes I feel like Sunny really loves me, that I'm more than a money source and that maybe she'd like things to be different between us. I'd like that, too, but neither of us seems to know what to do about it. I'm not making excuses for your dad or myself. I just don't know how to relate to Sunny—Jared either, for that matter. Whenever I try, it's a miserable failure."

Shiloh looked skeptical. "Maybe it's one of those things that gets better with practice."

"You're probably right, and I want to. The distance between us bothers me more than they'll ever know. And I imagine Jon is still regretting all those lost years, too."

"There's no need. I adjusted. Kids are pretty versatile. And though I may have sounded bitter a few minutes ago, I'm not. As I grew up, life had a way of teaching me things I only thought I understood. Only adults can truly understand adult problems and frustrations. Your kids will be a little more understanding when they face the same problems."

He took his eyes off the road long enough to meet her gaze. "I know that in this day and age, it's a fantasy dream, but I hope to God they never have to."

The doctor's office was tastefully, stereotypically decorated and full to overflowing with women, most in some stage of pregnancy. It seemed to Shiloh that every head turned when she and Cade entered the reception room. Unable to shake the feeling that everyone knew why she was there, she focused her gaze on the receptionist's window. Nonetheless, she was aware of the feminine glances cast Cade's way. Even the eyes of the women who looked as if they could deliver any moment held a glimmer of appreciation.

Shiloh couldn't help noticing that one middle-aged lady with fiery red hair and hard blue eyes seemed especially interested in their arrival. Unlike the others, who went back to their reading or handwork after a curious glance at the newcomers, this woman fixed Cade with an intense stare, as if she was trying to place him or get his attention—which she finally did.

"Why, Mr. Robichaux!" she gushed with a smile as sharp as the speculative gleam in her eyes. "How very nice to see you."

"Ms. Davenport," Cade said, the curtness in his voice bordering rudeness. From her spot at the receptionist's window Shiloh watched him move some magazines from the crowded sofa and sit next to a pregnant girl who didn't look over sixteen. Ignoring the woman, he picked up a magazine and opened it, shutting down the avenues of conversation. Strange. She didn't think rudeness was natural to him.

"Whatever are you doing here?" the redhead asked despite Cade's obvious reluctance in talking with her.

Shiloh had an intuitive feeling that the question would have been innocent coming from anyone else, but she could almost hear the real, unspoken question: *What are you, a single man, doing here in an ob-gyn office?*

"I brought a friend."

Handing the office help the insurance card she'd requested, Shiloh cast a quick look at the Davenport woman and saw that the woman's sly smile was fixed on her. Feeling like a chicken alone in the pen with a hungry fox, Shiloh turned away and accepted the clipboard with a medical form on it.

Cade rose when she turned, and offered her his place on the floral sofa.

"I'm fine," she said.

"Sit." The command was curt, but she knew it wasn't intentional. This Davenport woman had made him irritable.

A quick peek at the nosy redhead as Shiloh settled herself in the spot Cade had just vacated told her that the woman was uncommonly interested in her.

"Is this your—" the woman paused "—friend?"

"Yes," Cade replied, but he made no move to introduce them. Shiloh looked up at him with a frown. What was going on?

"Hello, dear," the woman said, rising and closing the few feet between them, her hand outstretched. "I'm Mavis Davenport."

Shiloh smiled and took the woman's hand in a politeness ingrained from childhood. "Shiloh Rambler."

"Rambler?" Mavis Davenport's countenance brightened, and her mouth fell open. "Are you one of *the* Ramblers? No, wait! Let me guess. You've got to be one of Jon's children."

Shiloh nodded. "I'm—"

"Shiloh? Right?"

"Right."

"I've got a wonderful memory for names," Mavis Davenport said, returning to her chair. "Shiloh Rambler." She cut her triumphant gaze to Cade. "Now isn't this just too fascinating?"

A quick look at Cade told Shiloh that he was furious. They were saved from any more questions by the nurse, who called Mavis Davenport's name and the name of the young woman sitting beside Shiloh.

Cade took the vacated seat and, crossing his arms over his wide chest, leaned his head against the back of the sofa and closed his eyes as if he wanted to block out the last few minutes.

"Who was that?" Shiloh whispered.

He cocked one baleful eye open. "No one who matters." He closed his eye again.

"I guess it's safe to assume you don't care for her."

He didn't even bother to look at her. "Safer than the FDIC."

The finality of his tone said that he had given Mavis Davenport all the time he was going to. Troubled by his reluctance to talk about it, but not wanting to press the issue, Shiloh took the hint and got to work filling out the form.

While Shiloh was seeing the doctor, Cade sat in the outer office, trying to concentrate on an article and failing miserably. A picture of Mavis Davenport's gloating face kept getting in the way. Mavis was a columnist for the *Thibodaux Sun* newspaper, ostensibly covering the area social events. What she really wrote was a gossip column.

She delighted in reporting any hint of scandal connected with the local citizenry, all cleverly worded so that she could never be accused of actually pointing the finger at anyone's indiscretions or excesses. She'd never be so crass. What she excelled at was planting ideas in the minds of the readers, ideas that urged them to let their imaginations run free. No one, not even the town's elite, was immune to digs from her poisonous pen.

Cade couldn't imagine anything more irksome than running into her like this. He had hoped she wouldn't jump on the fact that he was there with Shiloh, which was why he hadn't introduced them, but of course, that was the first thing she'd done. He hoped she accepted his explanation of why he was there; after all, it was the truth. Still, he hadn't liked the malicious light that had glittered in her eyes as she'd said, "Now isn't this just too fascinating?"

"I beg your pardon?"

The sound of the unfamiliar voice brought Cade's attention back to the present. He turned his head toward the source of the query and saw a very pregnant woman sitting next to him, a polite look of question on her plump face. He regarded her blankly. He had no idea what she meant.

"You said something was fascinating," she said as a reminder.

Damn! He must have been thinking out loud. "Uh, yeah." Desperate for an explanation, he tapped the magazine with his forefinger. "This article in here."

He glanced down at the cover and read the first one his gaze fell on. "How To Make Freezer Jam In Half The Time," he read.

The woman looked stunned. "You make jam?"

Only when she asked the question did he realize that he was digging a deeper hole. He shrugged. "Well, I . . . sometimes, yeah, if the little lady gets too busy, you know."

"That's wonderful!" The woman beamed. "If you'll excuse me for saying so, you don't look like the type."

"Uh, thanks."

Just then, the door to the inner rooms opened and Shiloh stepped out. He was so relieved he could have kissed her.

After taking blood and urine samples and giving her a physical examination, Ted Devane—who'd gone to college with Cade—had given her a due date of December twenty-first, a handful of pamphlets that explained some basic questions she might have, and prescriptions for iron tablets and vitamins. He had told her that the nausea was normal, but that her backaches and stomach cramps might be indications of a problem. But advising her not to borrow trouble, he said to get plenty of rest, told her not to worry and urged her to call him if she had any questions or needed anything whatsoever before she went back home. He scribbled down the name of a doctor in Chattanooga and wished her good luck.

Feeling more pregnant than she had so far, Shiloh reentered the reception room thirty minutes later. Cade was where she'd left him, reading a year-old issue of a popular woman's magazine. Thankfully, Mavis Davenport was nowhere to be seen.

He looked up as she stepped through the door. Did she only imagine the relief in his eyes?

"Ready?" he asked, rising.

"Yes."

Taking her elbow he escorted her out to the car. "How did you like Ted?" he asked, guiding the Bronco out into the traffic.

Shiloh looked up from one of the pamphlets she was reading. "Very much. He was thorough and seemed to have genuine compassion for all my aches and pains."

"He was always a sensitive type and very smart in school. I figured he'd make a good doctor."

Cade gave his attention back to the road and Shiloh resumed her reading. "Oh, my gosh," she said a few moments later.

"What?" he said sharply, glancing over at her.

She looked up at him, disbelief on her face. "It says here that at eight weeks, which is about what I am, that the baby is only one inch long but that it has recognizably human features." She went back to her reading.

Cade thought that she had never looked so beautiful as she did at that first moment when she came to a full realization of what was actually taking place inside her body. Wonder and awe lent a softness to her countenance and a glimmer of tears to her eyes. Knowing that he'd missed all the small joys and trials of Mary Rose's pregnancies, Cade experienced a sharp pang of regret.

"Amazing," he said, and meant it. It was a fact he hadn't known.

They drove the remaining distance to Rambler's Rest in silence. Shiloh was absorbed in her pamphlets, leaving Cade to his heightened feelings of guilt and isolation.

Chapter Six

"Oh, my God!" Garrett said, tossing the paper to the table and leaping to his feet. He stalked to the bottom of the servants' stairs that led from the kitchen to the second floor. "Shiloh!" he bellowed. "Get your sweet tush down her—now!"

Molly, who'd been putting a load of clothes in the washer when she'd heard Garrett's outburst, poked her head into the kitchen. "What is it?" she asked, her heart racing.

"That bitch!" Garrett grated lowly, banging his fist on the table so hard the flatware rattled.

"Shiloh?" Molly asked, amazed, wondering what had happened to make her husband turn white with fury.

"Not Shiloh. Mavis Davenport."

The odious name fell from his lips into the comparative silence of the room with the impact of an anvil being dropped from a penthouse roof. Considering the source, Garrett's feelings were right on target. Mavis Davenport had wreaked plenty of havoc in Molly's and Garrett's lives.

"What's she done now?"

Garrett picked up the paper and handed it to his wife. "Read it."

Before Molly could do more than locate the column, Shiloh entered the kitchen. She was wearing baggy shorts that made her look too thin and a black T-shirt that gave her complexion a paleness that underscored the dark circles beneath her eyes.

"What's the matter?" she asked.

Garrett pinned her with a gaze that was somewhere between annoyed and troubled. "Maybe you ought to tell me."

"Oh, Lordy," Molly said, drawing Garrett's and Shiloh's attention to her. She raised her head and looked up. "Shiloh, do you know who Mavis Davenport is?"

"No," she said with a shrug and a shake of her head. "But I met her yesterday afternoon."

"Oh, yeah? Where?"

She'd been wrong. Garrett wasn't annoyed. He was furious. And it had something to do with Mavis Davenport. Had the woman called Garrett and told him they'd met at the gynecologist's office? If possible, Shiloh grew more pale. She gave a sigh of resignation. There was nothing to do but tell them the truth. Her look of determined resolution encompassed both Molly and Garrett.

"Both of you had better sit down. I have some bad news."

In the space of a heartbeat the anger on Garrett's face was replaced by surprise and concern. Glancing in Molly's direction, he sat back down in the chair he had vacated earlier. Without a word and wearing a look of dread, Molly seated herself beside her husband.

Shiloh wrung her hands, but she met the wary expectance in their eyes directly. She drew a deep breath and blurted, "I'm pregnant."

For the span of several seconds there was no sound in the room. She could have sworn that everyone had stopped breathing. Then Molly turned to look at Garrett who heaved a great sigh—of relief?—and pushed back his chair, a wide smile on his face. Halfway across the kitchen the smile erupted into laughter.

Shiloh frowned. He wasn't angry anymore, she thought, as he put his arms around her and hugged her tightly. He wasn't going to give her one of his famous big-brother lectures. What had happened to change his feelings from fury to relieved laughter?

"What's the matter with you?" she mumbled, pushing against his broad chest. "Surely you don't think this is *funny?*

Loosening his hold on her, he leaned back and looked at her with eyes full of love and tenderness. "Oh, God, Shiloh, when you said you had bad news I thought I was going to lose you." He brushed the tousled hair away from her face. "You'd better get one thing straight, sis."

She gave him a bemused nod.

"Death is bad news. War is bad news. Incurable diseases are bad news. In the scheme of things, babies are not bad news."

The tension that had held Shiloh in its grip ever since she'd learned that she was carrying Jack's baby evaporated like drops of dew in the morning sun. For some reason, Garrett's reaction to the situation was more important than her parents'. Her love for him was reflected in the tears she swore she would not shed.

"Not even when they're not planned and their mother isn't married to the father and never will be?" she asked in a quavering voice.

Garrett shook his head. "Especially not then."

"Thank you," she whispered.

"I gather Jack wasn't thrilled." It was a statement, not a question.

Bitterness edged her smile. "By the time I found out about the baby, Jack had already made it clear that he was finished with me. He hadn't asked for me to fall in love with him, you see. And since he no longer wanted me, he sure didn't like the idea of a baby." Her lower lip trembled. "Oh, Garrett, I feel like such a fool, and I'm so scared."

"I know, babe," he said, folding her close again, "I know."

Shiloh didn't see Molly get up, but the next thing she knew, her sister-in-law's arms were around her too. "I'll help all I can," Molly offered.

Shiloh couldn't speak around the lump in her throat; all she could do was nod and hold on to them and the comfort and support they offered. After long moments, Garrett released her and stepped back. His eyes held a suspicious brightness, but he was still smiling.

"You okay?"

Crossing her arms over her breasts as if the simple gesture would keep her from flying into a million pieces, Shiloh nodded. "What do you think every-one's going to say? What will Dad and Mom say?"

"Who cares about everyone? And don't worry about Mom and Dad. They'll be fine," Garrett assured her. "They love you."

"I know they do, but Garrett, this is something that happens to fifteen-year-old girls, not grown-up, responsible women," she reminded him. "I know zilch about taking care of babies. How can I run a business with a baby on my hip?"

"This wasn't planned, then?"

Her look seemed to ask him if he was crazy. "Planned? Am I the kind of person who would deliberately add confusion and chaos to her life?"

"No, but you are getting older, and it crossed my mind that maybe you wanted a baby as much as you wanted Jack."

"I'd never get pregnant out of wedlock on purpose. Believe me."

"I do. So you are going to keep it, then?"

Shiloh's surprise was mirrored in her eyes. "Of course I'm going to keep it, even though Jack did offer me a tidy sum to have an abortion."

"That bastard!" Garrett bit out. "From that picture you showed me, he looks like the kind who would pay to keep his life nice and tidy."

"Which is something Shiloh's won't be again for about eighteen years," Molly said with an attempt at levity.

The ploy worked. Garrett laughed and in spite of herself, Shiloh smiled. "Just what I needed to hear."

Molly brushed the hair away from Shiloh's forehead, much as she would have for her daughter. "It's going to be fine. Motherhood is as natural to a woman as breathing. You'll be great. And as for Le Mirage, there are such things as baby-sitters and nannies, you know."

"I know you're right, but the whole thing is just so... overwhelming. You know, other than the sickness and the backaches to remind me, I do my best not to think about it."

"It isn't going to go away just because you ignore it, sis," Garrett said.

"That's what Cade said."

Garrett and Molly looked at each other. The mention of Cade's name reminded them of the newspaper article.

"Cade!"

"Damn!" they said simultaneously.

"What is it?" Shiloh asked, looking from one to the other. "What about Cade?"

"Mavis Davenport," Garrett said as if the name explained everything.

"Why do you keep talking about her?" Shiloh asked with a shrug. "I met her in the doctor's office yesterday—so what?"

"We know."

A frown puckered Shiloh's brow. "You know? How?"

"Shiloh," Molly said, "Mavis Davenport writes gossip for the local paper."

Shiloh's eyes widened. She had a sudden sneaking suspicion what had made Garrett so angry.

"Cut all the soft soap and let her read it for herself," Garrett commanded.

Wordlessly Molly handed Shiloh the paper. The column, complete with a photo of a smiling Mavis, was at the bottom of the page. There was news of an upcoming wedding shower, a description of a young lawyer's new home and then, at the end of the column, there it was.

"News Flash! Yesterday afternoon this reporter spotted a local self-made millionaire at a Thibodaux gynecologist's office in the company of the sister of a local rice farmer/entrepreneur. Could it be that the handsome and elusive bachelor made his recent purchase of an abandoned plantation because he's expecting to hear the patter of little feet in the near future?"

Shiloh looked up at Garrett and Molly, disbelief molding her features. "I can't believe it. That... that..."

"Bitch," Garrett supplied.

"Why would she print something like that?" Shiloh asked. "Everyone who lives around here will know exactly who she's talking about. What did Cade and I ever do to her?"

"Nothing," Garrett said. "Mavis Davenport thrives on mayhem and confusion, sis. If she can stir up some dirt about someone, her day is complete."

"Should I call Cade and ask if he's seen it?"

"It might not hurt," Garrett said. "But I don't want you worrying about this. I've had a lot of practice shutting Mavis Davenport up."

At Shiloh's questioning look, Molly launched into an account of the stories Mavis had written about her and Garrett before their wedding. She told Shiloh how Mavis had accosted them in the elevator of the Waverley Hotel and how she'd hinted of her pregnancy with Laura Leigh before Molly had even told Garrett the news. "She is not a nice person," Molly finished with a grimace.

"It sounds as if she's very unhappy."

"Leave it to Shiloh to have sympathy for the woman," Garrett said with an indulgent smile.

"Look, we can't change things. I'll call Cade and see if he's upset, but there's no sense in your calling her on the carpet about it. I agree that it was pretty tacky of her, but something juicier will come along in a few days and then this will be old news. Besides, I'll be gone soon, and it won't matter then."

The words were brave, but in her heart she was cringing.

Cade wasn't answering the phone all morning. He had turned on the machine in his office to pick up any business calls and ignored the phone's ringing in the house while he spent the morning outside with the landscape artists, as they euphemistically called themselves. Funny, he'd always considered them just yardmen.

By the time they left at noon, leaving a projected cost for everything he wanted done, he realized that their title was apropos...at least in their minds. He might have bought a nice McCarthy original for the price they wanted to charge him, but he consoled himself with the knowledge that the grounds had been allowed to deteriorate for several years, and it would take a lot of care to get them back into the shape he felt the plantation deserved.

He was heading for the house when Jared, driving like a madman, pulled his pickup into the driveway, screeching to a stop with a spray of gravel. Cade's heart slammed against his chest in sudden panic. Something must be wrong.

Jared flung open the truck's door and slammed it shut. He carried a rolled newspaper in his hand. Relief swept through Cade. Nothing was wrong; Jared was just thoroughly ticked off.

"Who put the burr under your saddle?" he asked with a smile.

Jared slapped the newspaper against Cade's chest, his face contorted with fury. "You did, you son of a bitch."

Confusion knitted Cade's brow; he automatically reached for the paper. "I don't know what you're talking about."

Jared planted his hands on his hips and thrust out his chin. "Well, read the paper. Improve your mind. I've already got it opened to a good spot. Mavis Davenport's column. Bottom of the page."

At the mention of Mavis's name Cade's blood ran cold. He didn't have to read the column to have a pretty good idea what it said. His heart beating in dread, he unrolled the folded paper and flipped it over to the bottom half of the page. It took only seconds to find the column and read the disparaging print.

Damn the woman to an eternal hell! It was just the sort of thing he would expect her to write. He wondered if Shiloh had seen it and what she thought of the Davenport brand of journalism. He'd give her a call as soon as he dealt with Jared...which might take some doing. After reading Mavis's sly comments, he could see that Jared's anger made perfect sense. Cade rerolled the paper and raised his steady gaze to his son's.

"Well, is it true?"

"Is what true?" Cade countered, sorry and a bit resentful that Jared had tried and convicted him without even attempting to find out the truth.

"Don't play games with me," Jared commanded, his manner insulting. "I'm not one of your damned computer programs. Did Mavis Davenport see you at the doctor's office with that Rambler woman or not?"

Cade's nod was slow, thoughtful. "She did."

If possible, Jared's face went even whiter than it had been. "She's pregnant?"

"Yes."

"You hypocrite," Jared condemned in a shaking voice. "Ever since Sunny and I were old enough to have a conception of sex, you've preached that it was wrong outside of marriage. And you said that if we couldn't keep from doing it, we should at least be responsible enough to protect ourselves and our partners. What happened, Dad? Did you get caught up in the heat of the moment and forget your condom? Why in the hell didn't you practice what you preached?"

It was all Cade could do to keep from slapping the smug contemptuousness from Jared's face. He faced his son's anger, varied thoughts and scenarios roiling in his mind. His first response was to attempt to explain the situation, to make Jared understand. It would be so easy to say that the baby Shiloh carried wasn't his, that Jack what's-his-name had fathered it. He could watch the disappointment leave his son's face in slow degrees, and then they could sit down over lunch, laugh over the misunderstanding and cut Mavis Davenport to ribbons with their tongues. So easy.

The problem was that Cade couldn't bring himself to say the words that would settle things between him and his son. He'd rather carry the burden of Jared's disillusionment and pain himself than have him think less of Shiloh. He didn't want to contemplate why Jared's opinion of Shiloh mattered.

"What's wrong, Dad?" Jared taunted when Cade made no move to defend himself. "All out of lies?"

"Lies?" Cade countered. "I've told you the truth. But sometimes even the truth isn't what it seems."

"Don't try to dazzle me with all that pop psychology crap. What other truth can there be?"

Before she died, Cade's mother had often complained that parenting was a thankless job until kids grew up enough to understand the complexity of adult situations and decisions . . . which was basically what Shiloh had said about herself and her parents the other day.

"You've got to figure that out for yourself."

"Yeah, sure. I'll get right to work on figuring out the real meaning of life," Jared said in a voice that reeked of sarcasm. "In the meantime thanks a lot for ruining ours."

"Ours?" Cade asked with a frown.

"Yeah. Mine and Sunny's."

For a moment Jared's anger abated and Cade saw sorrow and concern for his sister in his son's eyes. At the same time, the burden in Cade's heart grew heavier. Sunny. Damn. Things were bad enough between them. "So Sunny knows, too?"

"Knows? She's the one who called me at Bruce's and told me about it. One of Sunny's friends called and told her after her *mother* read it." Jared threw up his hands in a gesture of frustration and disgust. "Hell, it's probably all over town by now. How are we supposed to face our friends?"

"If they're real friends this won't matter. They'll stand behind you."

"That's easy for you to say."

Jared's selfish attitude set Cade's irritation on the rise again.

"Damn, son," he said with an exasperated shake of his head. "Do you think I live in a vacuum? That you and Sunny are the only ones Mavis Davenport's version of the truth will affect?" His disbelieving gaze bored into his son's. "Well, I've got another news flash for you. I have friends, too. So do Shiloh and Molly and Garrett."

"Shiloh deserves whatever she gets."

Cade was stunned. Where was the live-and-let-live attitude Jared and his cronies professed to have? Where was the it's-none-of-my-business position he claimed to take? "I can't believe your lack of compassion, Jared. But I guess it takes something like this to see what people are really made of, to see who really cares about us."

For the first time since Jared had arrived, Cade saw a crack in the armor of his anger. "What are you getting at?"

"I'm getting at the fact that we're a family. We ought to stick together. Instead of attacking me, you should stand up for me, be supportive. And if your sense of morality can't handle that, the very least you can do is take a good look at yourself and make sure the mote is out of your eye before you start worrying about the beam in mine."

The anger had left Jared's face; he shifted uncomfortably at the gentle reminder that he might not be guilt free, either. Cade found no satisfaction in reminding his son of his own hypocrisy.

"Are you accusing me of messin' around?"

"That's just it. *I'm* not accusing *you* of anything." Cade straightened his drooping shoulders. "As you're always so quick to remind me, this is a free country. You think what you will about me and Shiloh. But sometimes, son, there comes a time in a man's life when he has to do what he thinks is right and to hell with the consequences.''

Cade walked up the flagstone walkway that led to the door of the house where Mary Rose lived with her husband, Jared and Sunny. He hoped his ex-wife wasn't at home. He wasn't up to an interrogation. After the scene with Jared, he wasn't sure he was up to a confrontation with his daughter.

When Jared had gone—his frame of mind not much better than when he'd arrived—Cade had started to call Shiloh but knew he was much too upset over his talk with his son to deal with any other problems just then. How could Jared be so judgmental? Having grown up being gauged by his father's actions and his family's financial status, Cade had tried to pass on a sense of fairness to his children. He'd urged Sunny and Jared not to make snap judgments, to adopt a wait-and-see attitude when it came to making decisions about people and events.

Cade consoled himself with the hope that maybe he'd done better instilling those attitudes in Sunny. He'd get things straight with her before he called to see how Shiloh was taking Mavis's veiled insinuations. A sigh fluttered from his lips as he pressed the doorbell.

The door swung open and Sunny stood before him, dressed in tight shorts with lace around the bottom and a baggy shirt that somehow only emphasized the rounded curves beneath. She'd been crying. Despite her obvious distress, it crossed Cade's mind with something of a shock that she wasn't a little girl anymore. She was growing into a young woman, and a gorgeous one, at that.

He plunged his hands into the pockets of his form-fitting jeans and offered her a tentative smile. "Hi."

"Hi." Tears glistened in her eyes.

"I thought we should talk."

Lifting a slender beringed hand, she shoved a heavy swath of dark hair away from her tear-splotched face. "I don't have anything to say to you."

"Look, I know you're upset, but—"

"Upset!" she cried, the tears tumbling over the fragile dam of her eyelashes. "Why wouldn't I be upset? You've just ruined my life, that's all! How could you do this to me?"

The truth trembled on his lips. But that selfish *me* attitude, that eagerness to condemn without gathering the facts, stilled the words before they escaped. "I haven't done anything to you, Sunny."

"A baby, Dad! At your age! What am I going to say to my friends?" she railed.

Cade had had enough. He was thoroughly disgusted with both his kids. Disgusted and weary and angry. He backed away, holding up both hands, palms outward, as if to deflect her anger. "I've already taken a butt-chewing from your brother. I don't intend to take one from you. If you want to talk when you calm down, if you want to discuss this like the adult you're always claiming to be, you know where to find me." He turned and started down the steps.

"I suppose you plan to marry her?"

The question, which sounded like an unequivocal statement, hit Cade with the force of a kick in the gut. He paused at the bottom step. Marry Shiloh? The possibility hadn't crossed his mind, but to Sunny, his marrying Shiloh would be the logical, the honorable thing to do, considering the information she was dealing with.

"To tell you the truth, Sunshine, the thought never crossed my mind."

Sunny looked as shocked by the admission as Cade had felt when she asked the question. Cade turned and sprinted down the steps to the car. Framed in the doorway, Sunny watched him leave, fresh tears trickling down her cheeks.

Cade peeled away from the curb with a squeal of tires. It was all he could do to hold the car to the prescribed speed limit until he reached the edge of the city. For twenty minutes he hurtled down back roads like a man possessed. When a doe jumped out of a patch of woods and he had to hit the brakes to keep from striking her, he realized that his actions were childish—if not downright suicidal—and pulled the Bronco to the shoulder of the road.

Letting the engine idle, he gripped the top of the steering wheel, willing his anger to leave and trying to get a handle on his frustrations. It was hard to imagine how anyone could have done a worse job of parenting than he had. Was it because he hadn't been there day in and day out to reinforce the values he believed in? If he had it all to do over again, he'd...

What, Robichaux? What would you do differently?

Not work so hard, maybe. Give Mary Rose and the kids more of his time. He sighed. What was it the country song said? That hindsight was twenty-twenty? He raked a hand through his slightly curling hair and eased the Bronco back onto the secondary highway.

A baby... At your age. Sunny's words played through his mind. What was so terrible about having a baby at forty-one? It wasn't as if he was *old,* but he knew that kids, entrenched in the arrogance and invincibility of their youth, perceived him as aged. Certainly too old to start another family. Until they'd seen Mavis's article, they'd no doubt thought he was too old to indulge in anything that might be considered youthful activity—like sex. In spite of his disgust, his mouth twisted in a wry smile. If Sunny thought he was too old for sex, she ought to check his pulse whenever Shiloh Rambler entered the room.

Shiloh. Now that he'd had it out with his kids, he should drive over and see what this whole sordid ordeal was doing to her life. He blew a stream of air from pursed lips. Who would have believed that going with her to the doctor—a simple act of concern and consideration—would have such far-reaching ramifications? So much for being a Good Samaritan.

Shiloh met him at the front door. She wasn't wearing any makeup, and she looked pale and tired. Her short hair was mussed, as if she'd been running her fingers through it. The worry dwelling in the depths of her blue eyes was replaced with relief when she saw who it was. She tried to smile. She didn't quite make it.

"Are you busy?" he asked.

She shook her head and indicated for him to come in. "Molly's at the store, and I'm baby-sitting Laura. Where have you been? I've been trying to call all day."

"I was outside all morning," he explained, following her into the parlor. She didn't sit; he didn't, either. She wrung her hands, while Cade worked his fingers into the front pockets of his Wranglers.

"Have you seen the paper?" she asked.

His lips twisted into the semblance of a smile. "Yeah. I'm sorry. I never meant to cause a ruckus. I was just trying to show a little support."

"There's no need to apologize. I appreciate everything you've done for me. Mavis's little commentary made it necessary for me to tell my family sooner than I'd planned, that's all. I'm just sorry you were dragged into my mess."

He shrugged off her concern. "What did Garrett say?"

"Actually, he took it very well. So did Molly. Even my parents accepted it without giving me too much flak." Twin lines appeared between her eyebrows. "What about you? Did the kids see it?"

"Yeah."

"And?" she prompted.

"They were both pretty upset, but they know how Mavis is." He didn't offer any details, and the generality of his statement held no hint that he hadn't told them the truth. He wasn't sure why, but he didn't want her to know he'd taken the blame for her condition.

She sank into a wing chair, weariness and defeat in every line of her slender body. "I'm so sorry. Do you want me to go to Mavis Davenport and tell her you aren't responsible . . . make her print a retraction?"

"I do not!" he exploded. He leveled a finger at her. "You stay away from that woman. She's poison." The sternness left his face, and he sat across from her. "Trust me. It's no big deal," he lied.

"Not for me, it isn't. I'll be leaving in a couple of weeks, but you have to live here."

"I'm a big boy," he said. "Don't worry about me, okay?"

"Okay."

"Are you sure you can handle it?"

She drew in a shuddering breath and tried to smile. "Truthfully? I'm not sure. But I guess we'll see what I'm made of, won't we? As my grandmother Rambler used to say, if you want to dance you have to pay the fiddler."

Cade didn't sleep much that night. Cade tossed and turned, Sunny's words tumbling around in his weary brain. *A baby! At your age!* Something about the scathing remark really got to him. For some reason he was more upset to think that Sunny imagined he was too old for a baby than for her to believe he'd had an affair. What was wrong with having a baby at his age? He knew a lot more now than he had when his kids were small. He'd probably be a much better father now than he had been at twenty-two. Not that he was likely to have any more offspring after all this time— was he?

I suppose you plan to marry her?

The thought he'd tried to keep from surfacing couldn't be denied any longer. Why not? he thought. Why not marry Shiloh? Though it was true that he hadn't thought about it, it was a darn good idea. And the more he did think about it, the more appealing the idea became. For hours, he wrestled with the pros and cons and polished his arguments to her objections. Sometime near dawn he fell asleep, a peaceful smile hovering on his lips.

When Shiloh opened the door at eight the next morning the last person she expected to see was Cade.

She stepped aside so he could come in. "What are you doing out and about so early?"

His gaze swept over her short robe, lingering on her legs. She felt that familiar awareness rising in her.

"I wanted to talk to you."

Forcing her heartbeats to a regular rhythm, Shiloh gave her attention to the smile in his blue eyes. "Sure. How about some coffee?"

The smile moved to his lips. "Sounds good."

She led the way to the empty kitchen and, going to the coffeepot, poured a mug full.

"Where is everyone?"

She turned to face him. "Molly is in the shower, and Garrett went out into the fields early. What's up?"

Instead of answering, Cade crossed the room to stand in front of her. He was so close that the clean scent of his shaving soap tantalized her nostrils, so close that his broad shoulders blocked her view of the kitchen. Dark hair peeked from the V of his shirt. She clenched her hands into tight fists, fighting the almost overpowering urge to reach up and see if it was silky or crisp to her touch. Feeling light-headed in the face of his undeniable masculinity, she let her gaze drift up to his face, over his clean-shaven jaw, past his sexily shaped upper lip to those drowsy bedroom eyes. She wasn't expecting the earnest determination mirrored there.

"Do you have to go back to Chattanooga?" he asked.

Like the determination, his question took Shiloh by surprise. "Of course I have to go back," she said with a puzzled frown. "Why?"

"Don't go," he urged in a husky voice. "Stay and marry me."

Shiloh didn't answer. Couldn't. She wasn't sure she'd ever been so knocked off balance. Not even when Jack had made his position very clear about not wanting her love. A dozen questions raced through her mind, but only one made it to her lips. "Why?"

"Why not?"

A short burst of laughter escaped her. "I can give you several reasons why not, the first one the most obvious. I'm pregnant by another man."

"Then it stands to reason that you need a husband, someone to take care of you."

The tenderness in his voice was compelling. She'd be lying to herself if she said the idea didn't hold a certain appeal, she thought. Recalling the sacrifices he'd made for his family as a young man, she realized he was acting very much in character. It would be so wonderful to have someone to lean on, someone to be there with her, someone to share the changes that would affect her life the next few months. She was tempted . . . very tempted. But if she accepted for her own selfish reasons, it wouldn't be fair to Cade.

"It isn't your place to take care of me."

"If we were married it would be."

"It wouldn't be fair—"

He put his fingers over her mouth to silence her. They were warm. Callused. Gentle.

"Just listen, please," he said, his eyes filled with the need to make her understand. "I have this huge house that's way too big for one middle-aged bachelor to rattle around in. It needs people to enjoy its beauty, its history. It needs the patter of little feet."

At mention of Mavis Davenport's phraseology, Shiloh felt hot color steal into her face. Cade grew serious. "Like I told you before, *chère*, I'm lonely. I'm lonely as hell. I've been looking for Ms. Right for sixteen years and I haven't had much luck. Any hope I had of finding a woman who'll love me like crazy is fading every day. I don't want to grow old alone, Shiloh, and that's the truth. I want to share however many days I have left with someone."

"Why me?"

"Because I like you. I think you like me. We have a lot in common. I admire your strength and independence. Right now, at this point in your life, you need someone. I don't mind that. I even like that. But you aren't the kind of woman who would expect me to be her whole world. You said you aren't comfortable with the idea of having a baby outside of marriage...so marry me." He smiled that slow, sexy smile. "Besides, I owe you."

"For what?" she asked, a bemused expression on her face.

"You came to my rescue the summer I was accused of stealing hay. I think it's only fair that I repay the gesture by coming to your rescue. Besides, you'd be doing me a favor."

"I'd be doing you a favor? How?"

"I messed up my first marriage. I didn't do a very good job with my kids. Your baby needs a father. I'm willing to take on that responsibility from everything like ballet lessons or T-ball to college tuition. Maybe if I have another chance, this time I'll get it right."

"You're suggesting a marriage of convenience?"

"Sort of." There was complete candor in his blue eyes. "I know you're still in love with Jack, but as far as I'm concerned I'm talking about till death do us part."

"It would be a marriage in every sense of the word, then?" she asked, feeling her face flame. Lord! Was she seriously considering his outrageous suggestion?

He gave her a slow nod and the heat of a controlled desire crept into his eyes. Reaching out, he lifted her chin and brushed his thumb over her bottom lip. "You have to know that I want you ... that I've wanted you since the first day you arrived," he confessed in a husky voice. "If you wouldn't find it a hardship, I'd like very much to make love with you."

She did know how he felt. She'd caught glimpses of the same need she had experienced in Cade's eyes, but she'd been so guilty over what she considered her own shameless sexuality that she'd convinced herself that what she saw was her imagination.

"I'm in no hurry to consummate the marriage," he was saying now. "You have your baby and let your heart heal, and we'll go from there."

"What if one of us falls in love with someone else?"

One corner of his mouth hiked in a crooked grin. "I've been looking a long time, *chère,*" he told her. "If I haven't found the right woman in sixteen years, I'd say my chances of finding her any time soon are pretty slim. Of course, if you did fall in love and wanted out, I'd let you go."

What more could she want?

Love, a small voice inside her said. *What about love?*

What about it? Like Cade, she hadn't had much luck finding that elusive emotion. Maybe this was the way to go, after all. Friendship, companionship, a healthy sexual relationship. It was far more appealing than being alone.

"Can I think about it?"

He glanced at his watch. "You've got till six this evening."

"What's the hurry?" she asked, her eyes wide with surprise.

"I want to make an honest woman of you as soon as possible. It's the only way I know to stop the gossip." Before she could reply, he bent and dropped a brief kiss to her parted lips.

Even in those short seconds, Shiloh could tell that Cade Robichaux's mouth tasted divine. She suspected that sharing a bed with him wouldn't be a hardship at all.

Chapter Seven

When Cade left, Shiloh carried her juice to the table and sat down to think his offer through. Marriage. Not to Jack, but to Cade Robichaux. It was really strange; she'd never been able to picture marriage with Jack, even when she'd convinced herself that that was where their relationship was headed. She'd never been able to imagine them sitting across the breakfast table from one another or doing mundane things like watching TV or mowing the yard together. The only things she could see them doing together were dancing or going to some art exhibit. She couldn't picture him with a child at all.

It was different with Cade. She could easily see him sitting across from her in Magnolia Manor's spacious kitchen. Could see him cuddling the baby—Jack's baby—as he did Laura Leigh. It was very easy, and a bit painful, to picture him sprawled in a bed the two of them would share, his chest bare, the sheet draped over his lean hips.

She sipped at her juice and tried to ignore the now-familiar nausea. It was evident that Cade had given his proposal a lot of thought. He wanted this marriage and all it entailed, but did she? Was she ready to give up her independence and become part of someone's—a relative stranger's—life? Was she willing to give over half of the rearing of her child to a man who, by his own admission, hadn't done such a great job with his own?

And she still hadn't faced the most important consideration—was she contemplating Cade's proposal because to do so would make things easier on her? If she married him, she wouldn't have to bear her baby outside of marriage. It would have a name. She would have a wonderful place to live and bring up a child. She would have a handsome husband.

"You could do a lot worse," she said aloud.

"I thought I heard Cade's voice," Molly said, toweling her hair dry as she entered the room.

Wearing one of Garrett's T-shirts that was stretched over her belly, she looked ready to pop. Shiloh's hand went to her stomach, which was still relatively flat. How long before she got that big? "You did. He just left."

Molly glanced at the kitchen clock. "What's he doing out so early?"

"He came to ask me to marry him."

Molly's hands stilled above her head; then, as if she were in a daze, she lowered the towel. "He *what?*"

"Asked me to marry him."

"Why?"

"That's what I asked him," Shiloh said, drawing her finger through the condensation on her glass. "He says that we're both lonely, that I need someone right now and that his house has plenty of room."

"And what do you think of the offer?" Molly asked, sitting across from her sister-in-law.

Shiloh shook her head. "I honestly don't know. The advantages hold a certain appeal. I wouldn't have to risk running into Jack if I stayed here. That's something. My baby would have a name. We'll both have a nice home."

"What about love?"

"I thought of that, and Cade has, too. He doesn't think he'll fall in love at this point in his life. After all, he hasn't since he and Mary Rose split up. I haven't had much luck with it, either, and after my encounter with Jack I'm not sure I'm even interested in looking anymore."

"But a marriage of convenience!" Molly said.

Shiloh laughed, her pert nose wrinkling. "Oh, Mol! That's rich, coming from you. That's exactly why you and Garrett married. You both wanted to hold on to Rambler's Rest."

"But I loved Garrett," Molly said, defending her actions. "And Garrett didn't know it, but he loved me, too."

"Well, if Cade and I realize we love each other sometime down the road, it'll just be a little lagniappe." Shiloh's mouth curved in a bittersweet smile. "I'm not sure that love isn't a highly overrated emotion. In this day and age, having the same values and sharing a solid friendship stand a better chance of surviving a marriage than love, and there's a lot less chance of getting hurt. Just look at the old days. Most marriages were strong and many of them were marriages of convenience.''

"I can't argue that," Molly said. Her troubled eyes met Shiloh's. "It sounds as if you've made up your mind to accept."

"I'm not sure," Shiloh said. "What do you think I should do?"

"Oh, no, you don't!" Molly said with a shake of her wet head. "You're not going to pin the blame on me if this mad scheme doesn't work out." She reached across the table and took Shiloh's hand in hers. "I can't tell you what to do, but I will tell you this. Cade Robichaux is a good man, an honorable man, and I believe with all my heart that he'd be very good to any woman who shared his life."

"That's what I believe," Shiloh agreed. "I think we could have a satisfactory life together, a good life. Maybe even a happy life." She gave a throaty laugh. "And what the heck. I'm a Rambler, and Ramblers are a gambling sort."

When Cade pulled into his driveway an hour and a half later, Shiloh's rental car was sitting in the driveway. Had she decided already? His heart began to beat out a heavy, ragged rhythm. What would he do if she said no? What would he do if she said yes? Ever since he'd left Rambler's Rest he'd been tied in knots, wondering if she thought he was a fool—or crazy—wondering if she did decide to accept his proposal if he would be making the biggest mistake of his life.

As he pulled into the driveway she got out of her car and leaned against it, waiting for him. She was wearing a one-piece, brown-and-white-polka-dot outfit with a short split skirt. A white belt was strapped around her still-slender waist, and rose-tipped toe-nails peeked from white sandals. She looked stylish and gorgeous and cool. Nothing in her manner gave him a clue as to her decision. He pulled the Bronco to a stop and got out, glad he was wearing dark sun-shades. He didn't want her to see the uncertainty in his eyes.

"Hi," he said solemnly.

She clasped her hands behind her back. Her smile was brief, nervous. "Hi."

"I didn't expect to see you so soon."

She raised herself to her tiptoes then lowered her heels to the ground. "I didn't expect to be here so soon, but once I decided, I couldn't see any sense prolonging the agony."

Her word choice didn't sound positive. "No. I guess not." Cade took off the sunglasses and put them into the breast pocket of his short-sleeved cotton shirt. Whatever she had to say, he wanted nothing but truth between them. "And?"

"I'll marry you."

Expecting the worst, Cade wasn't sure he'd heard her correctly. "You will?"

"You haven't changed your mind, have you?" Her voice was tinged with panic. "I've already sold my restaurant."

"No," he assured her in a gentle voice. "I haven't changed my mind." Looking into her eyes, he reached out and took her hand in his. Carried it to his lips. Her hand trembled the slightest bit. Or was it his? "Thank you, *chère*. You do me a great honor."

The sincerity of his old-fashioned declaration couldn't be denied. "I should be thanking you."

"No need," he told her. "But a kiss to seal the bargain wouldn't come amiss." Before she could reply he lowered his head and pressed a light kiss to her parted lips. Her mouth was soft, sweet. And he thought that for one instant she returned the pressure of his lips. Brief though the kiss was, Cade knew that the time until Shiloh was willing to share his bed would be interminable. He straightened and put his arm around her shoulders, drawing her against his side.

"Let's go inside. We have a lot of planning to do."

Facing Cade's children the next day was one of the hardest things Shiloh had ever done. It wasn't every day that a man married a woman carrying someone else's child. He was saving her reputation, maybe even her sanity; he was offering her a new beginning, a new life, and yet, Cade had thanked *her* for accepting *his* proposal. This marriage would mean considerable change in Sunny's and Jared's lives, and Shiloh had the feeling that she would bear the blame for any problems those changes brought about.

She was still feeling a remnant of stress from her discussion with her parents. Ellen and Jon had taken the news of her pregnancy reasonably well, but hearing that she was about to embark on a loveless marriage was something else. Her mother's dire warnings of making "the biggest mistake of your life" still rang in her ears, but strangely, her father, like Garrett, had been more than accepting of the news.

Pretending to sip the drink that was starting to make her sick, she sneaked surreptitious looks at the Robichaux offspring and wondered what excuse Cade had used to get them to come over. Though she looked uncomfortable, Sunny was as gorgeous as her picture hinted and, if Jared would lose the perpetual snarl that curled his upper lip, he'd be every bit as handsome as his father. Shiloh herself was a nervous wreck. She would have been twice as nervous to know that he had demanded that they show up to meet her properly and, as he'd put it, "discuss the situation."

She was thankful when Cade returned. He sat on the sofa beside her and took her hand in his. Sunny gave a small gasp and Jared glowered. Shiloh tensed and her stomach lurched. She swallowed back the nausea. Barfing just now would not be a way to win friends and influence Cade's children.

"I wanted you both to come over today because I have something to tell you."

"You *are* going to marry her!" Sunny cried, her eyes wide with disbelief.

"Yes, I am," Cade said. "The wedding will be this Friday evening at seven o'clock at Rambler's Rest."

Jared swore.

"But this is already Monday," Sunny said.

"I know."

"I think I have plans that night," Jared said, his voice polite, civil. His eyes said something else. His eyes said he had no intention of coming.

"Cancel them." There was no compromise in Cade's tone or expression. "I expect you to both be there."

Shiloh could almost hear the "or else" tacked to the end of his commandment. Feeling like the proverbial bump on the log, she spoke up. "I'd like you both to be there, too. My family will be coming, and since you'll be seeing a fair bit of each other during holidays, it will be a good opportunity for you to get to know them. They're a lot of fun."

"We spend holidays at home with our mother," Jared said.

"I see." Shiloh felt Cade's fingers tighten around hers. "Well," she said with a false, bright smile, "at any rate, I'm sure you'll be seeing a lot of them through the years."

"We want the wedding to go as smoothly as possible," Cade told them. "Maybe the situation isn't to your liking, but I want you both to know that even though Shiloh will be the new mistress of Magnolia Manor and it will be as much her home as it is mine, you're both always welcome."

"Always," Shiloh assured them. She looked from Jared's chilly gaze to Sunny's troubled blue eyes and felt compelled to try to make amends. "I know this is a shock for you."

"You can say that again," Jared mumbled. Cade's angry look forbade him to say anything else.

"I want you to know that I don't aspire to becoming a second mother to you. And I have no intention of trying to alienate you and your father. What I would like is for us to be friends. If not now, then at some time in the future. And if that isn't possible, maybe we can at least show each other some mutual respect."

"That certainly isn't too much to ask," Cade said. "Sunny?"

"I suppose not."

Cade looked at Jared.

"Respect is earned," he said

Cade's eyes hardened. "Damn right it is, and at this moment, mine for you is at a low ebb."

Unable to face the fury in his father's eyes, Jared lowered his gaze. "Can we go now?"

Cade stood and went to the front door. Without a word, he opened it and flung it wide. Without a word, Jared and Sunny rose. Sunny flung a confused look toward Shiloh, who, unable to hold back her nausea any longer, rose and headed for the bathroom.

As they passed where Cade stood, he detained Jared with a hand on his arm. "We've had our differences in the past, son, but I've never been so ashamed or so disappointed in you as now."

Jared didn't answer.

"Did you go see about that job?" Cade asked, changing the subject with startling abruptness.

"Yeah," Jared announced, a triumphant look on his face. "I got it."

"Good, because you've gotten your last free ride from me."

Jared looked as if he'd been slapped in the face. "All because I won't accept the fact that you've been screwing around with that woman in there?"

The muscle in Cade's jaw tightened, and he met Jared's gaze squarely. "No. You said the other day that I should practice what I preach. Well, that's just what I'm going to start doing. You've heard how my sisters and I supported our family from the time we were kids and how important I think responsibility is. Well, you two have had it too damned easy. The way you've been acting has made me aware of how spoiled and selfish the two of you are. But there won't be any more spoiling from me. I can promise you that."

He glanced from one to the other. "Neither of you is too good to work. Your mother and I both do. It's high time both of you got a job and learned a little about responsibility and how to take care of yourselves."

Seeing the despair on Sunny's face, he halted his tirade. A tender-hearted sort, she had always been affected more by a scolding than a spanking. "That's it," he said, "except that I expect you both to be at Rambler's Rest at seven o'clock Friday night whether you like the idea of this marriage or not."

"Jared and Sunny are here," Molly announced, stepping through the door of the room where Shiloh was getting ready for the ceremony. "And Ellen and Jon just drove up."

The wedding was to be a small, private affair, with just immediate family and a few close friends, no more than fifteen people total. Julie Scott, Shiloh's former manager, who'd been thrilled at the chance to purchase Le Mirage, had flown over with her daughters from Chattanooga. Other than her family, Julie was the only person Shiloh had told the truth about Jack and the baby and Cade's offer of marriage. Julie and her daughters had arrived the night before, and all three had positively drooled over Cade.

"He's absolutely gorgeous!" Julie had said.

"He's not half bad, is he?" Shiloh had responded with a thrill of pride.

"Half bad? Honey, he looks all bad to me," Julie had said with a throaty laugh. "And that's just the way I like them. All man, all bad. Jack was just too pretty for my taste. Your little misfortune just may have turned out to be the best thing that's ever happened to you." She had given Shiloh a sisterly hug.

"I hope so," Shiloh said out loud.

"What?" Molly said, fluffing the short veil of the hat that matched the white linen suit Shiloh would soon don.

"Oh, I was just thinking out loud," Shiloh replied, pressing the flats of her hands against her abdomen and arching her back against the slight but nagging pain that had greeted her on waking that morning. "Is everyone here, then?"

"I think so." Molly frowned. "Are you all right?"

"I'm fine. Just a little backache." She tried to smile. "And a big case of nerves."

"You'll be fine," Molly said. "It's practically painless."

A knock sounded at the door and before Shiloh could answer a well-groomed, salt-and-pepper head appeared, a smile wreathing the features that were so similar to Shiloh's.

"Is this the bride?"

"Mama!" she said, her voice catching.

Ellen entered the bedroom in a swirl of taupe chiffon and perfume. Wearing a smile, she took Shiloh's hands in hers. "Let me look at you." Shiloh stood in silence while Ellen gave her the once-over. "You look wonderful," she pronounced at last. "Too thin, but wonderful."

Drawing a breath of relief that sounded more like a sob, Shiloh went into her mother's familiar embrace. "Oh, Mama!"

"Don't you dare cry, Shiloh Rambler," Ellen ordered, her own voice sounding curiously thick. "You'll make me start, and both of us will have to redo our makeup."

"Yes ma'am." Shiloh drew back with a tremulous smile. "Where's Daddy?"

"He's downstairs talking to your fiancé. Why on earth didn't you tell me he was so handsome?"

* * *

Cade extended his hand in greeting. "Good to see you, Mr. Rambler."

Jon Rambler, an older, somewhat heavier, replica of Garrett, took Cade's hand with a smile. "It's good to see you, too, son. You're looking well."

There was no doubt in Cade's mind that Jon was sincere. "Older."

Jon laughed. "We're all looking older. Garrett tells me you've done very well for yourself."

"I just lucked into something I was good at," Cade said, shrugging off his success.

"You always made it a habit to be good at whatever you did," Jon observed. "I hope you do the same with this marriage."

Cade knew that the statement was the reason behind Jon's seeking him out. As much as he knew the older man had liked him and had believed in him in his youth, he would still be responsible for Shiloh's future happiness.

"I know you're concerned, sir. Any father would be. But I can assure you that I only want the best for Shiloh and her baby."

At the mention of the baby, Jon Rambler's face looked grim. "She was pretty torn up, wasn't she?"

Cade nodded.

Jon straightened his shoulders and sighed. "She's always been a hard one to figure. Her mother's and my failures affected her far more than they did Garrett. I never felt like I gave her what she needed. I tried, but..." His voice trailed away.

"I know what you're going through," Cade confessed. "I'm having a problem relating to my kids right now."

Jon looked up. "I can't imagine you having kids. I'll bet they're upset over this marriage."

Cade plunged his hands into the pockets of his dark trousers. His smile bordered on cynical. "Oh, they're upset, all right, but mostly because they think the baby is mine."

"What!" Jon said in disbelief. "Why?"

"You saw something worth saving in me. If it hadn't been for you, I'd never have made anything of myself."

"I don't believe that for a moment. You have too much drive, too much ambition. You don't owe me a thing, Cade. You gave me an honest day's work for a fair wage."

"Thanks," Cade said. "But it's more than that. I feel like I owe Shiloh for that time she saved my hide."

"Owe her? Look, son, I don't want you to do this because you think you need to settle any old debts."

"I'm not. Not really."

Something in his eyes must have lent credence to his denial. Jon met his gaze. "Discounting your motive, why on earth would you let your kids believe the baby is yours?"

Cade could offer no reason except the one he gave himself. "I don't want them or anyone else thinking bad about Shiloh."

"You'd rather have them think bad about you?"

Cade's smile was tinged with traces of old pain. "I'm used to it. She isn't."

A slight breeze drifted through the garden, wafting the sweet perfume of half a dozen kinds of flowers through the air. Clusters of rambling roses dripped from arbors and trellises, their fragrant blossoms dancing in the wind.

The guests were seated in a semicircle around the sundial where Shiloh, Cade and the preacher stood. Cade clasped her hand tightly, as if he were afraid she'd change her mind and bolt from the garden.

Running was the farthest thing from her mind. For the first time in a long time she felt safe, secure, as if everything would be all right... forever. Besides, a woman would have to be mad to run from a man who looked like her soon-to-be husband.

She could hardly concentrate on the ceremony for looking at Cade, who was breathtakingly handsome in a dark tailored suit and white shirt. The lines around his mouth betrayed his tension, but there was tenderness in his eyes as they exchanged the age-old vows, promising to love and cherish for as long as they both lived, no matter what might befall them.

Her stomach cramped again, and a fleeting picture of Jack crossed her mind. The image of his handsome, brooding visage failed to elicit any tender feelings or even her customary anger. She wondered if she was getting over Jack, working through the pain of his rejection, letting go of her rage at him and herself... and knew that if all those things were true, she could thank the man standing beside her.

Shiloh looked down at the hand wrapped around hers. Considering that they were beginning their life together with a lie, she should have felt guilt, even fear. She might find Cade physically exciting, and he might want her, but they didn't love each other. How could they when they were virtual strangers? Still, she felt no guilt for making her promise to love him forever, or any fear for the uncertainty of her future.

"You may kiss your bride."

The minister's words broke the chain of her thoughts, and she lifted her eyes to her husband's. His eyes were smiling, and so were his lips...lips that swooped to take hers in a kiss so soft, so sweet, so full of promise that her heart soared like a bird freed from a cage. Then he drew away, and she was left with a hollow, aching feeling. Before she could brood on the sudden feeling of loss, the preacher presented them to the assemblage as Mr. and Mrs. Cade Robichaux, and they were caught up in the swarm of family and friends, hugs and kisses and wishes for a long and happy life together.

When things settled down, she and Cade opened their wedding gifts that included everything from a sexy nightie to a bread-making machine. They accepted the presents along with the good-natured—sometimes ribald—teasing.

Carried along on the emotion of the moment, Shiloh could almost believe that it was a real marriage, that the wishes for a long and good life together would come true...until her happy gaze fell on Jared and Sunny. They sat apart from the rest of the group, unwilling to share in any of the festivities, unwilling to even make a pretense that the wedding was anything but a sham.

When the gifts were all open and there was a lull while Molly and Ellen brought in the punch, Shiloh excused herself from the cluster of people and crossed the room to where her new stepchildren sat. Her heart was beating like crazy, and though she knew she should say something to them she didn't know what that something should be.

They wore wary expressions as they watched her approach, as if they, too, wondered what she would say or do. What she did was sit in a nearby chair.

"Thank you for coming."

"Sure," Jared said. Sunny didn't say anything.

Shiloh was torn between the urge to cry or to shake some sense into them. "It was a nice ceremony, wasn't it? And we got a lot of great gifts."

"Oh, yes," Sunny gushed, apparently aware that she couldn't just sit there and nod.

There was a challenging look in Jared's eyes. "I thought the nightgown and all the jokes about the wedding night were a bit redundant under the circumstances. Baby clothes might have been a better choice."

Shiloh's gasp mingled with Sunny's. The comment about the baby clothes was meant to hurt, and it had. But even through the shock of his blatant cruelty, Shiloh realized she had no idea what he meant about the gown and the prewedding-night teasing. "I beg your pardon?"

"Isn't it a little hard to pretend that tonight will be any different from dozens of others you've spent with my dad?"

Something clicked. Like the air after a storm, Sunny's and Jared's actions became crystal clear. She didn't know why, but she knew that the Robichaux offspring thought the baby she carried was their father's.

Why?

Hadn't Cade said that he'd set them straight about the column? It was a topic she intended to take up with her husband just as soon as they got back to Magnolia Manor, but right now it was imperative that she ease the pain reflected in his children's eyes.

"I think there's been a misunderstanding." She heard the trembling in her voice and cleared her throat. "I've never spent a night with your dad. I don't know why he led you to believe a lie, but he isn't the father of the baby I'm expecting."

Sunny looked shocked; Jared looked disbelieving. Shiloh forged ahead before her courage deserted her.

"I thought I was in love with a man from Chattanooga. I thought he loved me, too. I had dreams of marrying him." In spite of herself she felt tears gathering in her eyes. "But I was wrong about him. He didn't love me, and he didn't want to marry me...not even when he found out about the baby."

Sunny looked as if she was about to cry; Jared had the grace to look away.

Shiloh swallowed and blinked back the moisture gathering in her eyes. "I came down to visit my brother and try to figure out what to do. I saw your dad again, and he asked me to help him with his business dinner. Over the course of a week or so he figured out why I was sick all the time and, like the decent man he is, he offered to help me. He made the appointment with Dr. Devane and went with me for support."

That brought both their heads up.

"Mavis Davenport was there and she wrote that gossip column after figuring out that we were together. I thought he'd explained all this to you. I thought you knew the truth." She tried to laugh, failed. Caught her bottom lip between her teeth. "No wonder you dislike me so much. You thought I'd trapped your dad into marriage."

"Haven't you?" Though the look in Jared's eyes was no longer quite so condemning, there was still a hint of defiance in his eyes.

"I don't think so," Shiloh said with a slow shake of her head. "He had reasons for wanting to marry me, and I think you should discuss those with him. But your dad and I are adults, Jared. I have no hold on him other than that any old friend has on another. He asked me to marry him, not the other way around."

Sunny and Jared sat silent, trying to absorb this new information.

"Cade Robichaux is a very special person. He always was. Sometimes I feel guilty for being weak enough to accept what he's offered me. Sometimes I get really scared about the future, but we think it will be a good, workable relationship. I plan on doing my best to make him a good wife, and I promise that I'll always treat him with the respect and honor he deserves. The same respect and honor he should be getting from both of you."

"Oh, God, I'm so sorry!" Sunny said, two fat tears rolling down her cheeks.

Shiloh reached into her jacket pocket for the unused handkerchief, her "something borrowed" from her mother. "Don't cry," she said, pressing the lace-bedecked square into Sunny's hand. "Not now. It's supposed to be a happy time."

Before Sunny or Jared could comment, Shiloh heard Garrett utter a blistering curse. Startled, she looked up and, following his gaze, saw a woman round the corner of the house. One hand held a floppy hat to her flaming red head; a camera dangled from the other. Her high heels clicked on the flagstone path that meandered through the garden.

Shiloh's mouth fell open, and her horrified gaze found Cade's.

"Why, doesn't everyone look nice!" Mavis Davenport gushed, bestowing her malicious smile impartially among the guests. "I hope I haven't missed *everything!*"

Chapter Eight

Shiloh sat in the front of Cade's Bronco, pressing her spine against the seat in an effort to ease the pain in her back while she fought to hold her feelings of dejection and weariness at bay. What could possibly happen next? Ever since Mavis had crashed the reception, the gaiety had gone out of the evening. Reality had reared its ugly head, and it was a frightening thing to behold. Jared and Sunny had witnessed just how far the wretched woman would go to get a story, but they had also seen their father and Garrett—one on each side—escort the newswoman from the premises.

That fiasco, plus the realization that Sunny and Jared didn't know the truth, had burst Shiloh's fantasy bubble. It was hard to maintain the pretense of happily ever after when the hard, uncompromising truth dogged her at every turn.

The truth was that even though her marriage to Cade had given her a measure of security and had taken the edge off the scandal she was finding so hard to deal with, she had no guarantees that this marriage was any less susceptible to trials and tribulations than a made-in-heaven match.

The truth was that, for reasons that made little sense to her, Cade had sacrificed his already shaky relationship with his children by marrying her—and worse, leading them to believe that he was the father of her child.

The truth was, no matter how shallow it made her appear in her own eyes, or the eyes of others, she knew now that she'd been fooling herself. Cade had been right. What she'd felt for Jack hadn't been love at all, which is why getting over him was relatively easy. She didn't know what would happen between her and Cade in the future, but she knew she was terribly, shamefully drawn to him.

And if she was really truthful she'd admit that she wanted to don the sheer black nightie and use it and every feminine wile she possessed to make this wedding night a real one. A soft sigh escaped her.

"Tired?" Cade asked, his voice silencing her wayward thoughts.

She glanced over at the silhouette of his strong profile. "A little."

"Me, too." He shot a brief glance her way. "Can you believe the gall of that woman? How can anyone be so insensitive?"

"I don't know. As Garrett would say, she's tough."

"As nails," Cade agreed. "God, I hate to think what tomorrow's column will say."

The comment seemed the perfect opening to broach her troubled thoughts. "Cade?"

"Hmm?"

"Why did you let your kids believe you're the father of my baby?"

He didn't speak for several seconds. When he did, he kept his eyes focused on the highway unraveling before them. "They wanted to know if I was there with you, and I said yes. They wanted to know if you were pregnant, and I said yes. They didn't bother asking if I was responsible. They already had their minds made up. I was disappointed and ticked off because they were so damned intolerant, they didn't ask. So I just didn't bother correcting their assumptions."

"But why? This last week must have been unbearable for you."

"Better for it to be unbearable for me than you."

Just as she had instantly understood his children's actions at the reception, Cade's actions now became clear. He'd made the unselfish gesture for her. "Why should it matter how hard things are for me? Why should you care?"

"Why shouldn't I?" he countered. When she didn't speak, he said, "Look, don't go feeling sorry for me. I went into this with my eyes open. No one held a gun to my head. I don't have any regrets, and I don't want you to, either."

"How can I not have regrets? I made out like a bandit. I'm getting all the good stuff in this marriage, but you..." Her voice trickled into silence, and she shook her head in sorrow. "You're the one who's made all the sacrifices. You're the one who's getting the bad end of this deal."

"That isn't how I see it. Now can we shelve this discussion? It's done. We're married. It's too late to turn back the clock—okay?"

She nodded.

He pulled the car into the driveway and turned off the ignition. Then he got out, rounded the hood and helped her out. After the insulated quiet of the car, it seemed as if the crickets and frogs were each determined to outsing the other. It was a sound she had loved during her summers spent at Rambler's Rest, a sound she realized she'd missed. The serenity of the night eased the tension that had grown in steady increments after Mavis's arrival.

Shiloh drew a deep breath. An isolated thundershower had cleansed the country air, and the night was redolent with the mingled odors of damp earth, honeysuckle and magnolia blossoms that grew profusely on the giant trees that proliferated the yard. According to Cade, no less than twenty-four of the waxenleaved evergreens surrounded the house. When Conrad Krueger had built the plantation more than a hundred and forty years before, he'd named it well.

Taking her elbow, Cade helped her up the steep steps that led to the front porch. The massive carriage lights on either side of the leaded-glass door provided a warm welcome, as did the huge urns of variegated caladiums on either side. Shiloh thought how easy it would be to think of this house as home.

Cade opened the door, and she started through the aperture.

"Wait!"

She turned, a question in her blue eyes.

"I'm supposed to carry you across the threshold."

Her heart picked up its pace. "I didn't think you'd want to satisfy all the traditional conventions, since this is a rather unconventional marriage."

"*You* did, didn't you?"

Despite her flagging spirits and her weariness a smile flickered in her eyes. "Do you mean did I do the something old, something new, something borrowed, something blue routine?" Balancing on one stylish pump, she held up the other foot. "Right down to the penny in my shoe. After all, it's my first time."

"And your last time," Cade said. "All the more reason to do it up right." With that, he scooped her up into his arms. With a small gasp, partly of surprise, partly of pain, she flung her arms around his neck.

His eyes found hers. "Are you all right?"

At the concern on his face, she felt the prickling of tears beneath her eyelids. "I'm fine. Just a little backache."

"You have too many backaches," he said. "It doesn't sound right to me. I want you to call Ted Devane."

"I will."

She must have convinced him, because he stepped through the doorway and pushed the door shut with his foot. To Shiloh's surprise, he started up the stairs with her instead of setting her to her feet.

"What are you doing?"

"What do you think I'm doing?" he asked. "I'm carrying you upstairs."

"I see that you're going to be the kind of husband who wants to share everything," she said serenely. "How sweet."

"What do you mean?"

"If you carry me all the way to my room, I won't be the only one with a backache."

Cade's laughter was as intoxicating as a Mason jar full of moonshine.

"I'm reasonably fit . . . for my age," he said. "And carrying you is like carrying thistledown."

"More than reasonably, I'd say," Shiloh said and wished she could bite out her tongue. Why couldn't she just enjoy the teasing give and take and keep any personal thoughts out of her mind?

"Why, thank you, Mrs. Robichaux," Cade quipped, coming to a halt in front of her bedroom door. "That's very kind of you." He set her to her feet, started to straighten, uttered a groan and grabbed his back.

Shiloh's eyes widened. With a cry of alarm she reached out to steady him.

He cast her a roguish grin. "Just teasing," he said, straightening to his full six-foot-two-inch height.

She threw an ineffectual blow to his biceps. "Beast! You scared me out of a day's growth!"

"We can't have that. You're a shrimp now."

They stood smiling at each other as if everything was all right in their world, as if their relationship was a normal one and not one of convenience, as if theirs was a real marriage and not a sham.

Without warning her happiness began to fade and her mind resurrected the seriousness of the situation. "Thanks."

"For what?"

"For everything. Mostly for being you."

He gave a self-conscious shrug. "It's all I know how to be."

He dropped a kiss to her cheek, a fleeting, whisper-soft brushing of his lips near her ear. A delicious shiver rippled through her; she touched her cheek with her fingertips. Cade negotiated the few steps to his room across the hall. His hand was on the doorknob when she stopped him.

"Cade."

He turned his head to look at her, his eyebrows lifted in question.

She could feel her face flaming as she crossed the space separating them and placed her hand on his chest. His heart beat strong and steady. "If you... want me, I... I'd be glad to stay with you tonight."

"Why?"

"Because you've been so good to me... so understanding."

Cade took her hand in his and carried it to his mouth. His lips were warm on her palm. "Want you?" he growled in a low voice. "Sometimes I want you so much I ache with it, but I'm afraid I have to decline."

The look in her eyes said she didn't understand. "I don't want your pity, *chère*. Or your gratitude. When you can come to me because you want me, I'll be more than happy to oblige us both."

Tears of humiliation stung her eyes and she gave a short, embarrassed laugh. "I guess I'm doomed to making a fool of myself over the men in my life."

"No way. You're destined to be happy. I intend to make it a personal goal." He bent and kissed her again, this time on the mouth.

It was all she could do not to cling.

"Sweet dreams," he murmured against her lips.

She nodded and went back to her door.

"Shiloh..."

She looked over. "Yes?"

"I have a surprise for you tomorrow."

"What is it?"

His smile was as mischievous as a little boy's. "If I told you, it wouldn't be a surprise," he taunted. "Don't forget to call the doctor in the morning."

"I won't."

Cade closed his door and loosened the knot of his tie, pulling it from his neck and tossing it to the new chair that sat next to the antique highboy.

Idiot! he chided himself. What red-blooded man in his right mind—especially one who hadn't indulged his hormones in a while—would turn down an offer to sleep with a gorgeous, sexy woman...especially if that woman was his wife?

"You're losing it, Robichaux," he said aloud. "Definitely losing it."

He stripped off his shirt and slacks and peeled off his socks, sending them the same way as his tie. With the exception of Sunny's and Jared's behavior, the wedding had gone off without a hitch...until Mavis Davenport showed up. Damn the woman! How dare she just prance in there as if she'd been invited?

His mouth twisted into a grim smile. At least he and Garrett had gotten rid of her before she'd done more than make an appearance. Each had taken an arm and ushered her back the way she'd come. Though they hadn't used undue force, he could still hear her threats of assault ringing in his ears. Garrett had put a stop to that, though, retaliating with things like trespassing, harassment and slander suits. Still, there was no telling what the nosy witch would put in the morning paper.

Things had begun to fall apart after that. Nothing overt, just a lessening of enthusiasm, a dampening of spirits. Shiloh had seemed to wilt before his eyes, but it might have had more to do with how she was feeling than Mavis's unannounced appearance. He was worried about his new bride. It didn't seem right that she should be having backaches so early. He remembered Mary Rose complaining of them, but only when she was farther along—like Molly.

Cade turned off the window unit and opened the French doors that led to the *galerie*. Even when it was the hottest, he preferred sleeping with the room open, so that he could hear the night sounds and breathe the heavy, moisture-laden air. He went to the bed and crawled beneath the sheer mosquito netting, all that stood between him and the hungry insects that thrived in the sultry climate. Something about the diaphanous fabric reminded him of Shiloh.

She was so small and seemed so vulnerable, so...fragile, almost as if a good puff of wind would blow her away like the thistledown he had compared her weight to. Though she looked physically frangible, she compensated with an outward aura of self-sufficiency and toughness. Cade had the feeling that he was one of the few people who knew that her shell of invincibility was just that—a shell. He knew, because he'd had one too, for a long time.

Deep down, Shiloh was a mess of old hurts and ancient insecurities. Delaney's rejection and his refusal to claim his child hadn't helped any. But she would make it. The core of true steel that was the very heart of her would hold her in good stead. Though she was having a hard time adjusting to the idea of mother-hood, this baby would give her something, someone who would accept her for who she was, someone who would love her unconditionally. She needed that. Cade wasn't sure she could take it if something went wrong with this pregnancy.

He punched his pillow and folded his arms behind his head. Who was he trying to fool? He was the one who couldn't take it. He was scared to death that if anything happened and Shiloh didn't need him any-more, she would leave, and he'd be right back where he was a couple of weeks ago—alone, with no prospects for his lonely future.

It was a long, thoughtful night. Shiloh, who had put on the scandalous nightgown just because it was meant for her wedding night, was still awake at two in the morning, tossing and turning beneath her mosquito *barre*. The crickets and frogs still sang outside the open French doors, but their strident aria gave her no ease. Her stomach still hurt, and her back still ached. But most of her discontent came with the knowledge that when she'd said "I do" she'd embarked on a course that was uncharted and potentially rough.

How could she ever convince Cade's children that she wanted only the best for them? What had they thought of her confession? Sunny had seemed sorry. Had it made a difference in Jared's feelings for her? She sighed. Mavis had arrived before he could re-spond.

And how could she ever do enough to thank Cade for the sacrifice he'd made for her?

She drew herself into a ball in an effort to ease her pain, but she did not cry. She thought about the baby that she and Jack had made together and wondered why one man was able to give up so much and why the other was unwilling to give up anything. She wondered, as she drifted off to sleep, if Jack Delaney ever even thought about her and his child.

Cade was already up when Shiloh, clad in shorts and a T-shirt urging everyone to Save The Rain Forests, stumbled barefoot into the kitchen the next morning.

He looked up from the paper he was reading. "Good morning."

"Morning." She raked a hand through her short, tousled hair and stifled a yawn. "What does the paper say?"

Wordlessly, Cade handed her the section with Mavis's column. To Shiloh's surprise, the mention of the wedding was only slightly scathing.

"Last evening, in a garden ceremony with a smattering of friends and family in attendance, local computer whiz Cade Robichaux was married to Shiloh Rambler, sister of Rambler's Rest's Garrett Rambler and daughter of Jon Rambler, who lost the plantation several years ago in a much-publicized divorce. The bride, who looked a little pale to this reporter, wore a white linen suit with a snug-fitting jacket. The groom was sartorially splendid in a black suit and a scowl. Could there already be a 'little' trouble with the match?"

"She got her digs in, didn't she?" Shiloh said, tossing the paper aside and reaching into the refrigerator for the orange juice.

"It could have been worse," Cade reminded her. "Did you notice the quotation marks around 'little'?

I suspect she was referring to the baby and the possibility that it might be causing problems between us.''

"What a—"

"Bitch," Cade supplied, just as Garrett had the day of the other column.

"I'm inclined to agree. Did you catch this about my jacket being snug? I suppose she's implying that I'm showing already." Shiloh glanced at Cade sharply. "Am I?"

"Nary a bulge." His gaze moved over her still-slender body, and he wiggled his eyebrows. "Except in all the right places, of course."

The look in his eyes snatched her breath and set her heart to beating like a bird trapped in a cage. She started for the coffeepot to refill his cup, dragging her hand though his shower-damp hair as she passed. "Pervert," she quipped.

In an involuntary gesture, Cade's arm snaked out and caught her around the waist, halting her forward momentum and drawing her back until their eyes met. She could feel the hardness of his thigh against her leg. Could see the unabashed longing that sprang into his eyes.

His hand slid to the swell of her hip in an action that was as natural as the drawing of his next breath. "You ain't seen nothin' yet, *chère*."

The implication sent a rush of soft rose to her cheeks. Suddenly they were both aware that they had again fallen into an easy, teasing camaraderie, a camaraderie that held a potential risk.

"Would you like to see your surprise before breakfast?" he asked, switching topics in an effort to ease the awareness growing between them.

Disappointment mingled with Shiloh's relief. "I'd love to see my surprise."

"Come on, then," he said, rising and taking her hand.

He led the way to the bottom of the stairs and sprinted up them, Shiloh close on his heels. Though she was tired from her sleepless night, there was no denying the hint of excitement his secrecy engendered.

At the top he said, "Close your eyes."

Shiloh did as he commanded, carefully putting one foot in front of the other as he led her to his "surprise." It seemed as if they'd covered at least a mile, though she knew they'd only traversed the hall a few feet.

"Okay. You can open them now."

Her lashes swept upward. She was in the room that adjoined hers. It occupied the east corner of the house and looked out over the lawn and the bayou. A recipient of the sun's first rays, it would be cheerful in the morning and saved from the direct afternoon sunlight. At the moment it was empty except for three items: a dapple-gray rocking horse that boasted a basket on either end for passengers, a wicker perambulator with a hanging umbrella over the top, and a Grecian-style cradle.

Shiloh crossed to it, eagerness in every step. Kneeling beside it, she ran a caressing hand over the delicate turned spindles. Pure pleasure emanated from her face as she looked up at him. "Where on earth did you find all this stuff?"

"In the attic. They need cleaning up and maybe a little paint and varnish. And, of course, the umbrella fabric needs replacing."

She went to the rocking horse and swept her finger-tips over the flowing lines of the carved mane. "This is wonderful!"

"The one rocker on the horse needs a little repair, but other than that, it's in pretty good shape."

Shiloh's eyes smiled into his. "It's all just...perfect. It was considerate of you to think about the baby."

"Considerate?" he denied. "Nah. I'm just a cheapskate. I found it and figured it would save me from having to buy those expensive reproductions."

"Liar," she retaliated. "You knew I'd love it."

"I hoped you would," he said in all seriousness.

Breathless from the sudden warmth in his eyes, she pivoted on her heel and went to the window. "This room would make a great nursery, wouldn't it?"

"That's what I thought. I've already had the floors and woodwork refinished. All you'll have to do is pick out your colors and whatever baby things you need."

She turned from the window and leaned her hips against the sill. "It's too far away," she confessed with a shake of her head. "I can't even begin to think about any of that just yet."

"Do you plan on finding out what it is?" he asked.

She considered that possibility a moment. "I think I'd rather be surprised."

"But what if you paint the room pink and have a boy?"

"I'll paint it white and play it safe." She turned to him. "I can bring in my bright colors with pictures, rugs and blankets. What do you think?"

Uncertainty flickered in Cade's eyes. "You're asking me?"

"You will be this baby's father, you know."

"I know, but hearing you talk about it as if it's already fact sort of took me by surprise."

"I know." She crossed the room and stood on tiptoe to plant a kiss of thanks to his smooth-shaven chin. "Thanks for being so thoughtful."

"It's my pleasure."

They started to leave the room, but Cade stopped her. He looked uncomfortable. "I need to ask you something."

"What?"

"At the reception last night Jared cornered me and asked if he can spend the summer here with us. He says he needs more freedom than Mary Rose is willing to give him. I told him I'd have to clear it with you."

"You don't have to clear it with me. It's your house. He's your son."

"True. But it's your house, too, and you're my wife, and Jared hasn't been very nice to you in the past. If you think his being here will be unpleasant in any way, I'll tell him to forget it."

Shiloh looked up into Cade's eyes, trying to find a clue as to what he was feeling. Was this a test of some kind? Was he trying to see how she would react to his children? No. She didn't think so. Though she knew that he would jump at the chance to get closer to his son, he was being honest about not wanting her to be inconvenienced or upset in any way.

"I can get along with Jared, if Jared can get along with me," she said. "Sunny is welcome, too."

The corners of Cade's mouth lifted in a slow, sweet smile. "That's what I figured you'd say. I'll go call and tell him to pack his stuff and come on over."

There was a buoyancy to his step as he started from the room. Halfway to the door he stopped, retraced his steps and, lifting Shiloh's chin, dropped a kiss to her parted lips before heading to the exit once more. Shiloh watched him go, her fingers pressed to her throbbing mouth, a bemused expression on her face.

The next two weeks passed in lazy summer splendor. Shiloh finalized the sale of Le Mirage to Julie and made arrangements to have her things packed and shipped from Chattanooga. She and Cade talked about the rest of the renovations and decorating, and he left much of the actual selections up to her. She found herself running back and forth from Magnolia Manor to Thibodaux several times a week. She supervised the workers, cooked delicious meals for Cade and haunted the antique and secondhand stores for bargains that would lend just the right touch to the house.

Though Sunny had thanked them for the invitation, she elected to divide her time between both households, a decision Shiloh could see herself making at that age. She was beginning to see that Sunny held a lot inside, just as she had. She also noticed that Cade's daughter did her best to juggle her time and attention between her parents, as if she was afraid that giving one of them more than the other might cause a major upheaval . . . or at least some hurt feelings.

Two days after Cade had secured Shiloh's permission, Jared moved into a downstairs bedroom lock, stock and stereo system. Shiloh couldn't complain about his choice of musical styles; his taste was eclectic—everything from Billy Ray Cyrus to Harry Connick, Jr., with a little Yanni, Cocteau Twins and Kenny G thrown in for good measure.

The problem was that whatever he listened to, he listened at a decibel level that sent Cade's Australian blue heeler scrambling under the porch. At those times, Shiloh stayed outside as much as she could. Molly teasingly told her to be glad Jared's tastes didn't run to heavy metal and that shattered eardrums were a small price to pay for goodwill. Maintaining goodwill was one reason Shiloh elected not to say anything about the music. Jared wasn't friendly by any stretch of the imagination, but he had lost his sarcasm and was at least polite. She didn't want to rock the boat, plain and simple.

"That was Sunny," Cade said, cradling the receiver and scraping a hand through his hair.

It was the evening of their two-week anniversary, and so far Shiloh didn't have any complaints about married life. "I thought it must be. Is something wrong?"

Cade looked surprised. "No. But she wants to have a party out here. We have more room than her mom and Michael. It just doesn't seem fair for me to ask you to put up with this on top of taking in Jared."

"Jared isn't any trouble, and I don't have a problem with Sunny and some of her friends coming over."

"Thirty-plus friends?"

"I made a living cooking for people, remember?"

"Are you volunteering to do the food? Sunny wondered if you would, but I was afraid to ask."

Shiloh pursed her lips prettily. "I can, and I will, but I have this sneaking feeling I've been manipulated."

The teasing light left Cade's eyes. "Let me re-phrase that. Since Mary Rose isn't much of a party person, Sunny would like for you to help her put this together. Would you like to help her and do the food? And more importantly, do you feel up to it?"

The question made her realize that just then she felt really good, something she couldn't claim to have felt in a long time. Her nausea lessened every day, and for once she hadn't been plagued with one of her nagging backaches...which, she didn't want to admit to Cade, seemed to be increasing in frequency and intensity.

"I think I'm up to it."

"Are you sure?"

"I'm sure. When does she want to do it?"

"Next Friday night."

"That gives us a week. If Sunny and I put our heads together we should be able to come up with something suitably ostentatious."

"Ostentatious?"

"Sure. She'll want this to be the most rad party of the summer, one all her friends will aspire to outdo." Shiloh grinned. "We'll let them break their hearts trying."

Cade laughed. "I'll tell Sunny you said you'd be glad to help."

Shiloh knew that Cade couldn't act as a buffer between her and the kids forever. If they were ever to grow closer, they would each have to make an effort. "No," she said, "I'll call her later on and see if she can come over tomorrow to help with the plans. We need to get rolling."

"Good enough. If you don't have anything pressing right now, would you like to go for a walk?"

The unexpected invitation was a pleasant surprise. A thunderstorm had passed through earlier in the afternoon, breaking the oppressive grip of heat and humidity that had held Thibodaux and the surrounding area hostage the past ten days.

"I'd love to," she said. "Let me go up and change my shoes."

Mere minutes later she found Cade waiting at the back door. Side by side they went down the steps and headed toward the narrow gravel road that led past the dovecote and the remaining slave quarters.

Cade indicated the fields that were dotted with rectangles of freshly baled hay. A tractor pulled a long flatbed trailer, and two young men were hefting the bales of coastal to the trailer while two others stacked it. Shiloh was afraid that the rain had ruined the hay.

"Brings back a lot of memories, doesn't it?" Cade asked.

"Yes," she agreed. The most vivid memories were of him—shirtless, clad in faded, skintight Wranglers that were wet with sweat around the low-slung waist, his slightly curly hair wet with the perspiration that ran in rivulets down his face and glistened on the rippling muscles of his arms and back like oil on water.

"It isn't very good hay," Cade said. "It has a lot of weeds and hasn't been fertilized in years—but this guy said he'd cut it for it, and it beat paying to have it bush hogged."

"Do you think the rain ruined it?"

"He's using it to feed cattle. It'll be all right." He indicated a line along the bayou. "Next year I'd like to plant some cotton and put in a hundred acres of alfalfa down along the bayou."

Shiloh pulled the feathery top out of a stalk of Johnson grass that grew along the fence line and lifted it to her mouth to chew on, something she'd done innumerable times in her youth. "That sounds like a good idea. There's always a market for good alfalfa."

Cade plucked himself a sprig of grass. "I'll talk to Garrett. Have him come over and test the soil. He can tell me what my best bet is."

"How much land is left in the plantation?"

"Almost six hundred acres," he said, moving his piece of grass to the other side of his mouth. "More than I can say grace over, but I'll be damned if I'll sell any of it off."

"I don't blame you."

They walked along fences that needed repairing and past the barn that had once housed the Krueger stables. They passed dog kennels where one Krueger son-in-law had kept nearly fifty fox and coyote hounds, and ended up at an open tree-rimmed spot along the bayou that was approachable by car. Someone had been there recently. Tire tracks had beaten down the tall grass, and beer cans littered the ground. A pair of pink panties hung from a tree branch.

"Obviously a popular place," Cade said, removing the flimsy undergarment with a stick and tossing them into the rain-swollen waters of the bayou. He started walking again. "I'll pick up the trash later."

Shiloh skipped along beside him to keep up with his long-legged stride. "You know, this spot reminds me of that place at Rambler's Rest. The one where you took Pamela Hardy that night." Too late, she realized that recalling that night and Pamela's rejection of him might bring back unwanted memories.

Cade rubbed a palm over his whisker-stubbled chin, a sheepish look on his face. He kicked at a beer can, cut his gaze toward her and grinned, that sexy smile that sent her libido into overdrive. "Yeah, except I think I was drinking Wild Turkey instead of Miller."

She let out a breath of relief. He wasn't upset. "Whatever happened to Pamela, anyway?"

His smile broadened. "Good old Pamela changed her tune when I came back and she realized that I'd made some money. She called and offered to escort me to a Parents Without Partners shindig...since I was new in town and everything."

Walking backward, Shiloh danced along a few paces ahead of him, her smile reaching from ear to ear, her nose crinkled in delight. "You're kidding!"

He crossed his heart with his forefinger. "I swear."

"Did you go?"

He shook his head.

"What did you say?"

"I can't repeat it in front of a lady," he said with mock seriousness.

"Ca-ade! Come on! Tell me!" As she took another backward step her sneaker came down in a slight grassy depression filled with water. Before he could answer, her foot slipped out from under her. Her arms pinwheeled in awkward circles as she struggled to keep from falling. Just when she thought the battle was lost, she felt his arm go around her and pull her against his hard chest.

The combined scents of cologne and man assaulted her nostrils. She could feel the roughness of denim against her knees, could hear the sound of her suddenly racing heart. Desire, unexpected and breathtaking in its intensity, stormed the ramparts of determination she'd erected around her heart—a flimsy defense that had been hastily erected the moment she realized that her heart was vulnerable to Cade Robichaux's particular brand of seduction...which was no seduction at all, really, just Cade being himself.

Her breasts, already tender from her pregnancy, ached with the need to feel his touch. Afraid to break the spell of awareness holding her, knowing she should, she drew back and looked into his eyes. In spite of his comments about not wanting her pity, in spite of his speech about wanting her to be over Jack, there was no denying that Cade was experiencing the same feelings running roughshod over her resolve.

Passion clouded the blue eyes looking down at her. Instead of releasing her, he threaded his fingers through her short hair and planted his booted feet apart, drawing her with the strength of his gaze and the gentleness of his touch into the V of his legs. She started to say something, anything to stop the madness holding them in its grip, but when she opened her mouth to speak, the words were taken captive by his open mouth.

He tasted divine—like chicory-flavored coffee and breath mints. His kisses were sure, his lips firm, yet incredibly soft. His tongue dipped between her lips and he drank from her mouth like a thirsting animal, or a hummingbird long starved for its sustaining nectar. Knowing it was foolish, Shiloh gave him every bit of sweetness she had to offer.

She felt a lessening in the pressure of the fingers tangled in her hair and felt one hand trail with feather lightness down to her throat to rest on the pulse pounding there. Never taking his ravenous mouth from hers for longer than a second, he moved his hand to the buttons fastening her blouse. The first succumbed to his nimble touch. The second. And third. When he pushed the flowered fabric aside, she felt the touch of the breeze caress her bare shoulder. Longing for his touch, Shiloh had the fleeting thought that she really should start wearing front-closure bras.

That small factor proved no deterrent to Cade. She felt the warm roughness of his fingers when he slipped them beneath the satin and lace binding her and scooped the plumpness of her breast from its fragile casing. She gave a soft gasp and sagged against him. His thumb rubbed her already tender nipple to aching hardness. Her breasts felt full, heavy; they needed something to ease the pain.

As if he could read her mind, he ducked his head and captured the tip of her breast in the heat of his mouth, plumping her flesh upward and kneading the softness while his tongue lashed her with calculated expertise. She was wrong. It didn't help the ache at all. Instead, it was exquisite torture. Madness. Heaven. It felt as if there was a direct connection from her breast to the melting, throbbing core of her womanhood. Every tug of his lips on her nipple produced an answering chord of longing deep inside her.

Twining her fingers in the loose curls of his hair, she clutched his head closer, reveling in the feel of his mouth. At last, breathing heavily, Cade raised his head. Needing his nearness, Shiloh pressed her lower body against him in brazen abandon and contacted the heart-stopping hardness of his arousal.

Nothing this side of heaven could have kept her from touching him. A sound resembling a low growl rumbled up from his throat, and he moved against her trembling, questing fingers.

Without warning a long bleating sound from the direction of the hay field infringed on the silence of the bayou. Cade froze. Shiloh's breathing stopped. The sound came again. Someone was honking a horn. Thankfully—regrettably?—the noise shattered the mood building between them. Cade straightened. Remorse was fast replacing the passion in his eyes. He was sorry!

Embarrassed at having lowered her guard and mortified at what he must be thinking of her, Shiloh buried her teeth in her bottom lip and turned away to straighten her clothes. She fought the urge to give in to the tears she'd vowed not to shed. Lowering her head and her gaze, she started to cover herself. The tip of her breast was still wet from his mouth, still ultrasensitive. Ashamed of her behavior, she tugged the lacy covering up and jerked the front of her blouse together.

She had no chance to fasten the buttons before she felt the heaviness of Cade's hands on her shoulders. He turned her to face him. Still clutching her blouse, she looked up at him. Tears shimmered in her eyes.

"I'm sorry," he said.

"You don't have anything to be sorry for," she told him with false bravado. "You didn't exactly push yourself on me."

"Didn't I?"

She shook her head.

Heaving a sigh, he nudged her hands aside and began to refasten her buttons. "We should wait," he said. "For a lot of reasons."

"I know." Her voice shook.

"We have a lot of time. Forever."

She tried to smile. Nodded.

"We need to get to know each other." He grinned crookedly. "In other ways, I mean."

"Yes."

He finished the last button and, shifting his weight to one leg, rested his wrists on her shoulders. His smile was slow and lazy and as intoxicating as hard liquor. "She never called back, you know."

Shiloh had no idea who he was talking about. Her brows drew together in puzzlement. "Who?"

"Pam Hardy."

Shiloh realized he was trying to ease the tension binding them by reverting back to their earlier, light-hearted conversation. "Some people are such snobs," she said, doing her best to match his mood.

"Your family never was," he observed, trailing one knuckle down her heat-flushed cheek. "Maybe that's why I liked you all so much."

She looked up at him, sincerity radiating from her eyes. "I liked you, too. I still do."

"The feeling's mutual, Mrs. Robichaux, ma'am," he said with a tender smile.

Gratitude filled her aching heart. Shiloh wondered what she'd done to deserve being rescued by such a good man, a man it was becoming increasingly easy to imagine spending forever with. "You don't know how grateful I am for what you've done."

"No, *chère*," he said, his manner dead serious. Was that forever she saw reflected in his eyes? "It's you who doesn't understand how grateful I am."

Chapter Nine

Though her back was aching somewhat the next morning, Shiloh met her stepdaughter at the door with a smile. "I know it's Saturday, and you probably like to sleep in, but I thought we should start kicking around some ideas."

"I don't mind," Sunny said, stepping through the leaded-glass door and looking around. "Wow! This place is starting to look great."

The unexpected compliment sent a ribbon of pleasure unfurling through Shiloh. "Thank you. Your dad and I are discovering we have similar tastes, which makes it nice when he gives me carte blanche on the decorating." She inclined her head toward the kitchen. "Why don't we sit in the kitchen? I'd be glad to fix you a late breakfast if you like."

Sunny looked as surprised by the offer as Shiloh had felt at the girl's compliment. "No, thanks. I usually just have coffee."

"Ah, a woman after my own heart," Shiloh said, leading the way through the house. "I'm not supposed to have it right now, and most of the time the very thought of it makes me sick, but sometimes when I think I can't stand it a minute more, I steal a sip or two."

Sunny smiled . . . a real smile, Shiloh noticed.

"When I was a baby, my mom's mom used to give me sips of her coffee. Mama said I was hooked by the time I was walking, and I'd go around and drain any dregs left in any cup I might find sitting around."

They shared a moment of genuine laughter that seemed to erase the last traces of uneasiness that lay between them. Shiloh poured Sunny's chicory-laced coffee, which the girl doctored with lots of sugar and cream, and got herself a glass of grape juice. Fetching a couple of pens and yellow legal pads from a desk in what would one day be the library, she offered one to Sunny and seated herself across the table.

Then she took a deep breath, determined to get the bad stuff out of the way first. Sunny looked at her expectantly.

"Before we get started, I want to make one thing clear. I know there have been some changes since I grew up, but I'll bet it's still considered cute to sneak booze into a party. I want you to know that your father and I are agreed that there is to be no alcohol allowed. If either of us sees any, whoever brings it in will be asked to leave."

Shiloh couldn't read the expression in Sunny's eyes, but she rushed on before any objections were raised.

"We're not trying to be mean or act like old fogies, but you are minors, and there are laws. If someone got hurt or—God forbid—something worse happened, your dad could be held liable. He could lose everything he's worked so hard for."

"I hadn't thought of that," Sunny said. "I guess I never realized."

"Most kids don't. I know I didn't. Fortunately, I was lucky." Shiloh hoped that her indirect way of saying that she hadn't been squeaky clean in her youth would make a difference in the way Sunny perceived the situation.

"That's fine," Sunny said. "I'll tell everyone. If they bring it and get caught—so be it."

Shiloh smiled her approval. "Okay," she said, looking at her stepdaughter with unconcealed enthusiasm, "now that we have that out of the way, what kind of party did you have in mind? The theme you choose and the number of guests you invite will determine your decorations and what kind of food you serve."

"I hadn't thought about a theme," Sunny confessed. "I was thinking about a swimming party."

"Well, you certainly don't have to have a theme. It was just an idea."

"It isn't that I don't like it, it's just that I've never done this before."

Both Shiloh and Sunny were aware that each was going the extra mile to keep from offending the other.

"What did you have in mind?"

For the next hour and a half they kicked around ideas. When they finished discussing everything from a Hawaiian luau—no one would like the food—to a pirate theme—too corny—they decided on a plain old summer beach party theme with volleyball, music from the fifties and sixties and good old-fashioned hamburgers cooked on the grill.

So much for something different, Shiloh thought, glad that the session was at an end. At least the food preparation would be simple. She made a note to herself to check with the record stores about the availability of the music.

"I guess that's that," she said, placing a hand in the small of her back and arching it against the pain that had increased along with the stomach cramps that had started an hour or so before.

"I really appreciate your time," Sunny said.

"No problem." Shiloh winced as a particularly hard cramp hit.

"Are you okay?"

Shiloh tried to smile and didn't do a very good job of it. "Actually, I'm not feeling very well. I'm not trying to run you off, but would you mind if I went upstairs for a while?"

"Of course not," Sunny hastened to assure her. She looked embarrassed. "I just wanted to tell you that I'm sorry if I behaved badly toward you. It was just such a shock when I saw that write-up in the paper and then Dad said you two were getting married."

"I understand your feelings, Sunny, and I know how hard it is to share a parent. I went through this several times."

"You did?"

Shiloh nodded. "It must be even harder since you've had your dad to yourself all your life. I want you to know that I meant what I said the other day. I don't want to come between you and any of your family. I just want to make a place for me and the baby."

Sunny nodded and twisted a strand of hair around her index finger. "May I ask you something?"

"Surely."

"It may not be any of my business, but what happened with you and the baby's father?"

"He lied to me," Shiloh said without so much as a pause. "Not in so many words, but in actions. He gave me the rush and courted me with all sorts of fancy gifts and thoughtful gestures. I thought it meant love, but it didn't. When I told him how I felt, he made it very clear that all he wanted was a no-strings relationship."

Sunny looked thoughtful.

"When I told him about the baby a couple of weeks later, he was adamant about wanting no part of it or me. He wanted me to have an abortion. That may be the right decision for some people, but it wasn't right for me."

"I'm so sorry," the sixteen-year-old said, and Shiloh could see that she meant it.

"So am I, but his loss is my gain. I came down here and met your dad again, and he offered to help me." There was a tender light in her eyes as her thoughts turned toward her new husband. "He was willing to lose the respect of his family and his friends just to make things easier for me. That takes a special kind of man."

Her concerned gaze probed Sunny's. "I know your mother has talked with you about sex, but there's a lesson here, Sunny. If you're as smart as I think you are, you'll learn from it."

Sunny nodded. "I already know that a lot of guys don't mean everything they say. A lot of them don't mean *anything* they say."

"You got it. Be careful who you trust with your heart and your body. In time, a heart will mend. Someone new will come along and you wonder what you ever saw in anyone else. But sometimes in a physical relationship you get more than you bargained for, and too many times it's the woman who carries the scars. She's the one who has to face the world with her mistake. She's the one whose life will change, whose freedom, if she's a caring, nurturing person, will be gone forever."

"Do you feel as if you've lost your freedom?"

"In some ways, yes. But I'm lucky. I got your dad and I think he'll be a big help when the baby gets here. The bad thing is that not every woman can have a Cade Robichaux in her life."

"You care about him, don't you?"

Shiloh felt her face grow hot, but she forced herself to meet Sunny's questioning gaze. "Yes."

"Do you think you'll ever fall in love with him?"

Shiloh thought of Cade's hard physique, his slow, sexy smile, his gentleness and take-charge attitude. How could a woman not fall for him? "I think," she confessed in a moment's honesty, "that falling in love with him would be a very easy thing to do."

When Sunny left, Shiloh went upstairs to the bathroom and was shocked to find a smear of blood on her panties. With panic rampaging through her, she looked up Ted Devane's number and punched it out with trembling fingers. Suddenly she recalled the promise she'd made Cade on her wedding night—the promise to call Ted about her backaches, a promise she'd forgotten to follow through on.

The nurse said that the doctor was with a patient, but when she heard Shiloh's symptoms, she instructed her to lie down with her feet elevated until the doctor returned her call.

By the time he phoned thirty minutes later she'd worked herself into a frenzy of fear.

"Just calm down," Ted said, his mellifluous voice soothing her tattered nerves. "Is the cramping bad?"

"Not as bad as it was before I lay down," she said. "But my backaches seem to be more frequent lately. Cade wanted me to call you, but I just got so busy trying to settle in."

"I understand. Tell you what. You spend the rest of the day and all day tomorrow in bed. Give me a call late tomorrow afternoon and let me know how you feel. In the meantime if you get worse in any way—the cramps or spotting or your back—you get to my office immediately."

"Am I going to lose the baby?" she asked, her heart heavy, her eyes smarting with tears.

"Of course that's a possibility, but we're going to keep a close watch on you. From everything you've told me, this pregnancy has been rough emotionally, and I'm a firm believer that our mental health affects our physical well-being. Now that you've married Cade, you have new and different pressures on you."

Everything he said was true. Shiloh felt her panic abate a bit.

"You just slow down and take it easy. Stop running back and forth to town so you can have the house perfect for that dinner party of his. As a matter of fact, I'd postpone the dinner party. I think that once you stop worrying about everyone else and start taking care of Shiloh, you'll start feeling better.''

"I hope so.''

"Me, too. So stay in bed, and I'll give you a call later to see how you're doing.''

"All right. Thanks, Dr. Devane.''

"You bet.''

Shiloh hung up and undressed, donned a T-shirt and slipped back beneath the crisp percale sheets. She drew up her knees and tried to sleep, but sleep was a long time coming.

Shiloh was awakened by the sound of the doorknob rattling. Rubbing at her eyes, she rolled to her back. Cade stood in the doorway. A frown knitted his forehead, and worry shadowed his blue eyes.

"Are you okay?''

She raised herself to her elbows. "I think so.''

He stepped through the doorway and crossed the room, taking a seat on the edge of the bed. "What's the matter? Did Sunny say something to upset you?''

"Sunny!'' Shiloh's genuine surprise overshadowed the slight pain that still throbbed in her side. "Of course not! As a matter of fact, we got along better than I expected.''

His sigh of relief was audible. "Thank God. She can be difficult at times.'' Giving his attention to Shiloh's pale face, he reached out to lay his palm against her forehead and then her cheek in a parental gesture as old as mankind. "Are you sick, then?''

Though she did her best to keep them at bay, Shiloh felt her eyes fill with tears. "Not exactly. By the time Sunny and I finished, I had a really bad back-

ache, and I was cramping again. When I came upstairs I was spotting.''

Cade's face grew ashen. "Did you call Ted?"

She nodded and brushed the tears away with her
fingertips. "He told me to go to bed for a couple of
days, and if my pain or the bleeding gets worse, I'm to
go in to the office. He thinks that I'm doing too much
and that I've been under too much emotional strain.''

"You have been pretty busy the last two weeks. I
want you to forget about this house. And I'm calling
Sunny to tell her that the party is off until you're better." He started to rise, but Shiloh caught his arm.

"Cade, no! I can't let her down that way.''

"You won't be letting her down. She'll be disappointed, but she'll understand.''

Shiloh's eyes held a pleading he found hard to re-
sist. "Please.''

His jaw tightened.

"Let me do what Ted said and see how I feel tomorrow afternoon. If I'm still in a lot of pain, we'll
call it off.''

"How are you going to get things ready for the
party if you're in bed?"

"There won't be that much to do. Sunny doesn't
want anything fancy. She's doing the inviting, and I
have my lists made out for the food and decorations.
If you don't mind, you can pick up the food." She
gave him a tentative smile. "I hoped that if worse
comes to worst and I'm still in bed on Friday, maybe
I could sweet-talk you into grilling the hamburgers.''

Cade shook his head and a reluctant smile claimed
his lips. He reached for her left hand and toyed with
her wedding band. "You're something, you know
that?"

She laced her fingers through his and returned his smile. "Is that a yes?"

"Sure, I'll grill the hamburgers. I'd love to."

"Sunny would love it, too."

They looked down at their clasped hands and slowly looked up at each other. The tenderness in his eyes ripped away the last of her resistance. The feelings she'd had for Jack paled into insignificance when compared to those Cade ignited in her. And it wasn't just his looks or the way the bottom dropped out of her stomach when he smiled. It was his goodness, his steadfastness, all the kind and generous traits that made him the man he was.

Shiloh looked into her husband's eyes and faced her fate as bravely as she could. From the first day she'd seen him sitting on the front steps of Rambler's Rest, Cade had swept into her life, granting her no quarter when it came to letting her brood on past mistakes. From the moment he'd asked her to cater his dinner party, he had invaded her life and bombarded her skimpy defenses with his smile, threatening, despite her fears, to take her heart captive.

She'd lied to Sunny when she'd said that falling in love with Cade would be an easy thing to do. The truth was that whether or not he wanted it, whether or not she liked it, he'd won not only the battle but the war. The real truth was that she'd already fallen in love with him.

True to his word, Ted called to check on her that evening. Though she told herself that her back was better the next day, she started spotting again, and the doctor confined her to bed for another two days. By Thursday evening she was ready to climb the walls, and it was a foregone conclusion that even though the sporadic bleeding had stopped and the backache was nominal, Cade would have to pick up the slack for the party the next day. Sunny was understanding, even worried, when she came into Shiloh's room to tell her she hoped she would be well enough to at least get up and mingle with the guests.

When Friday morning dawned almost pain-free, Ted allowed her to get up and ramrod the last-minute preparations from the sofa or a chair, as long as she kept off her feet. Sunny was a nervous wreck; Cade was a rock. Even Jared stuck around after work, helping Cade however he could. Though he said little more to Shiloh than he hoped she was feeling better, Shiloh intercepted several measured looks from Cade's son.

At his dad's request, Jared had been assigned the task of watching for unnecessary roughhousing in the pool, and any smuggled booze. Though Jared would probably be the one doing the smuggling on any other night, Shiloh had the feeling that he liked being one of the authority figures.

By the time the guests started arriving, Shiloh's backache had returned. Not wanting to let Sunny down, she tried to stay off her feet while she smiled and shared the spotlight with Sunny and Cade as hosts. Cade insisted that she take advantage of a lounge chair while he fixed the hamburgers, but he didn't have to insist too hard.

Even though she wasn't feeling well, she had a good feeling about her first outing as a stepparent. If all the compliments about the house and the food were any indication, she'd passed the test. She didn't even mind the few curious stares that had raked her body.

She enjoyed listening to the golden oldies and watching the kids swim and dance and flirt. Their actions brought back memories of a time when life was simple and relatively carefree. As the night aged, there was less swimming and more dancing. Less laughter and more low conversations. Less rock songs and more slow ones, so young bodies and long golden limbs could brush against each other in a socially acceptable way. It was easy to see the subtle pairing off of couples.

From her spot deep in the shadows of the *galerie*, Shiloh, whose pain had eased for the moment, watched with a half smile while Sunny danced to Conway Twitty's "It's Only Make Believe" with a tall, dark-haired boy who owned a set of admirable shoulders and a narrow waist.

"Do you feel like dancing?"

Shiloh turned toward the sound of Cade's voice. He was standing a few feet away, looking as handsome as any of the teenaged boys in his plaid shirt, jeans and sneakers.

It wouldn't have mattered if pain racked her from head to toe. There was no way she was going to pass up a chance to be in her husband's arms—if only for a few moments. She swung her feet to the floor and felt her abdomen protest with another sharp pain. "I'd love to dance."

Cade held out his hands; Shiloh placed hers in them. He drew her to her feet and the pain screamed through her, all the way up to her shoulder. She bit back the gasp that sprang to her lips and went into his arms. Instead of the traditional dance form, he lifted both of her arms to his shoulders and wrapped his around her, pulling her against his hard, exciting length.

Shiloh looked up at him. The semidarkness hid the expression in his eyes, but his body spoke eloquently to hers as they danced...if that's what one would call what they were doing. They hardly moved. His arms held her closely, securely. She could feel the strength of his thighs brushing against hers with every shuffling step they took. Cade's nearness and the palm-sweating, heart-pounding sensations running riot through her almost negated the pain spiraling throughout her body. Almost.

Cade never stopped moving as Conway's song ended. It seemed as if the nocturnal noises created a melody that only the two of them could hear. Soon the plaintive refrains of "Put Your Head On My Shoulder" began to drift on the nighttime breeze. Succumbing to the plaintive plea, Shiloh rested her cheek against Cade's chest. She felt sixteen again. Sixteen and crazy in love.

When Paul Anka pleaded for the unknown girl to put her lips next to his, Cade abandoned the pretense of dancing. Shiloh looked up at him, a question in her eyes. But there was no need for a question. She knew he was going to kiss her as surely as she knew that, barring the end of the world, the sun would rise in the east the following morning. She saw his head dip nearer and lifted herself on her tiptoes to meet him halfway.

A pain, sharper than any so far, knifed through her, making her cry out, making the darkness around her grow even darker, making Cade's face waver and fade. She heard him call her name, but she couldn't answer. She felt herself sway like a sapling before a high wind and realized on some level that she was wilting to the wooden floor of the *galerie* like an uprooted flower left too long in the sun.

"Shiloh!"

Cade's voice called to her from the other end of a long tunnel. She struggled against the chains of darkness and forced her eyelids to half-mast. Cade knelt beside her. "You fainted, *chère*. What is it? Your back?"

As weak as a newborn, she clutched at his shirt-front, her nails digging for purchase of the pain. Her eyes flooded with the tears that overflowed her heart. "Oh, Cade," she wailed in a low, tear-thickened voice. "I'm afraid I'm losing the baby."

As if she weighed nothing more than the thistle-down he claimed, Cade scooped her up into his arms and strode toward the French doors that led to the parlor, bellowing for Jared as he went.

By some miracle, Jared was in the house. He appeared from the hallway, a look of query on his face. When he saw Shiloh in his father's arms, the question turned to shock.

Shiloh closed her eyes against another wave of pain and darkness, a single thought surfacing through her agony: Cade's kids would never forgive her for embarrassing them and messing things up this way.

"What's the matter?" Jared asked, striding alongside Cade.

"I'm taking Shiloh to the hospital."

She raised leaden eyelids. "I don't want to go to the hospital," she murmured.

"Well, that's too damn bad, *chère*," Cade drawled in a tone of voice that hovered somewhere between fear and bravado and sounded like sarcasm. "Jared, find Sunny and tell her what's happened. Get these kids out of here. I'll call you from the hospital as soon as I know something."

Shiloh forced herself up from the blackness. "Cade—"

"This isn't negotiable, Shiloh," he said, pushing the front screen open with his shoulder and striding out onto the porch where another group of kids was clustered.

"Jared," Shiloh said, reaching out blindly.

She felt his fingers close around hers. "Ma'am?"

Shiloh's pain-glazed gaze found his. "Will you tell Sunny that I'm so sorry I ruined everything. I'll try to make it up to her."

Jared didn't speak. He only clamped his jaw together tightly and nodded.

Satisfied that she'd done all she could to try to make amends, Shiloh gave herself over to the pain. She heard Cade's sneakers thumping down the wooden steps. Somehow, he opened the passenger door and deposited her gently inside. In a matter of seconds the tires of the Bronco were spewing pea gravel as he peeled out of the driveway.

Shiloh was aware of the car door slamming. Of hers being jerked open. Hot air blasting her. Being lifted into a gentle embrace. Doors sliding open and the blessed coolness again. Voices and confusion and the sound of crepe-soled shoes squeaking on the floors. And bright lights that danced around her in psychedelic splendor. Somehow she knew that Cade was carrying her. The voices came and went with her consciousness.

"About three months pregnant."

"...miscarriage..."

No! Not my baby.

"Ted Devane ... stat."

She was being laid gently on a hard table. She forced her eyelashes upward. Cade stood behind two nurses who looked like Mutt and Jeff. Their faces wavered before her tear-wet eyes. "I think I'm going to throw up," she said, curling into a fetal position in an effort to ease the pain.

"Here's a basin, Mrs. Robichaux," the nurse's comforting voice said while fingers probed her abdomen. "If you need to throw up, just go right ahead."

Shiloh nodded.

"She's clammy and her stomach is hard as a rock, June."

"I'm sorry, Mr. Robichaux, you'll have to step outside for a moment."

Shiloh realized that they were covering her with a sheet. Her shorts and panties were peeled off. She felt the sharp prick of an IV needle.

"She's bleeding some," a voice said. "I think she's going into shock. Get her blood pressure."

Shiloh felt the tight band of the blood pressure cuff around her arm. On the other side, no-nonsense fingers held her wrist. Tension molded the nurse's face, but she couldn't work up enough concern to wonder why before she faded out again. And in ...

" ... pulse is fast, and her abdomen is rock hard." Shiloh heard a familiar sound that she equated with the pumping of the rubber bulb and the hiss of released air that soon followed.

"See what's keeping Dr. Devane, June."

"I'll see."

"While you're seeing about that, see if you can round up an OR and an anesthesiologist. The bottom just fell out of her blood pressure. She's hemorrhaging internally.''

The tall nurse hurried out of the examination room without stopping to tell him anything. Something was very wrong. Cade paced the hall and leaned against the wall, his anguished eyes lifted to the ceiling. He heard the nurse's shoes on the floor and saw her approaching, another person who must be a lab technician in tow. For all her professional demeanor, there was no hiding the anxiety in the nurse's face.

"Excuse me," he said.

The nurse, whose name tag said June Brady, didn't even slow down. "What's going on?" he demanded.

"Dr. Devane and the anesthesiologist are on the way," the woman said, never stopping her long-legged stride. "We're going to cross-type her for a blood transfusion. We're going to have to operate."

Cade felt the blood drain from his face. "Operate? B-but she's pregnant."

"We're dealing with an ectopic pregnancy, Mr. Robichaux."

"Ectopic?" he echoed.

The R.N. stopped outside the examining-room door; the technician stepped inside. "A tubal pregnancy," the R.N. explained. "The egg gets lodged in the tube, which usually ruptures by three months and causes internal hemorrhaging. That's why her blood pressure has dropped so dramatically. Now if you'll excuse me, I have some instructions from the doctor." Without another word, she started through the door.

"Wait!" Cade took her arm. "She's going to be all right, isn't she?" He didn't like the catch he heard in his voice.

"It's pretty serious, Mr. Robichaux. Time is of the essence." She looked pointedly at his detaining hand. Cade released his hold on her and she stepped through the doors that separated him from Shiloh. He got only a glimpse of her lying pale and still before the door clicked shut.

How could this have happened? he asked himself. Surgery. The word tasted bitter in his mouth. Serious, the nurse said. The tube had ruptured and she was bleeding internally. God.

Please, God, let her be all right.

The door opened and the two nurses pushed through, guiding the gurney that carried his heart on it. Like an automaton, Cade stepped out of the way. Brushing past him, they wheeled the gurney down the hallway toward an arrow pointing the way to the operating room.

What should he do? Where should he go? Disoriented, he turned blindly. The baby, gone. Shiloh in shock, bleeding.... Truths, possibilities and scenarios that were worse than any horror movie he'd ever seen swirled like flotsam in the whirlpool of his thoughts. His gaze fell on a clock. Twelve-ten. It was hard to believe that an hour ago he and Shiloh were dancing. Hard to believe that he was about to kiss her. Would he ever have a chance to kiss her now? Dear Lord! The thought of losing her was unbearable, because...

"I love her." The realization settled into his mind like a benediction.

"Did you say something, Mr. Robichaux?"

Blindly he turned, seeking the source of the voice.

"If you're wondering where to go to wait, just follow the arrows. The waiting room for surgery will be down the hall on the right."

"Thank you." Brushing the moisture from his cheeks, he turned and stumbled down the hall, following the course the nurse had pointed out. She was right. The waiting room she'd told him about was just where she'd said it would be. Like a man looking for a port in a storm, he headed in that direction.

He was halfway to his destination when another sign caught his eye. He didn't even hesitate. Instead of going to the waiting room with its vending machines and its collection of old magazines and weary people, he turned the doorknob and stepped into the quiet peace of the chapel.

He sat down on the second pew of the hospital chapel and rested his forehead on his arms that were crossed on the back of the seat in front of him. *Dear God, please... please...*

He prayed, but he wasn't sure what he was praying for. Please what? Keep Shiloh safe? Don't let things be as bad as they sounded? Don't let her die? God, not that. Surely God wouldn't be so cruel as to take her away... not when he had waited sixteen years to find her....

Cade didn't have to be told that there was no saving the baby. Jack Delaney wouldn't have to worry about Shiloh making any demands on him now, wouldn't have to worry about a stranger showing up one day in the future and saying, "Hi, Dad."

A new and staggering thought entered Cade's mind. What about *his* future? Without the baby, Shiloh would no longer need anyone to take care of her, to shield her from the gossipmongers. She wouldn't need a father for her baby. Or a husband. Would she want one? Would she want him?

Time passed. He was never sure how much. Cade prayed that God would let Shiloh learn to love him. But if she couldn't fall in love with him, he added hastily, that was okay as long as she got well. He would give her up, let her go... give her her freedom if God would just let her be all right.

You can't bargain with God, son. The sound of his mother's voice came so clearly, he lifted his head to see if she stood somewhere nearby. But the room was empty. As empty as his aching heart.

Chapter Ten

It hadn't taken Jared long to clear the house and grounds of guests and lock things up. Sunny had listened while he explained what had happened. When he passed on Shiloh's apology, his sister had burst into inconsolable tears. She hadn't wanted to go to the hospital with him, and she'd been scared to stay at Magnolia Manor by herself, so he'd dropped her off at their mother's house. Then he'd driven to the hospital, parked in the emergency-room parking lot—his dad's Bronco was still there—and gone inside.

He looked around and controlled a shiver of apprehension. Hospitals gave Jared the creeps. They were too still, too sterile. Though his intellect told him that hospitals were there to help people get well, he never entered one without thinking about all those who *didn't*.

This thing with Shiloh and her baby was his closest brush with death. His dad's parents had died before he was old enough to understand, and his mom's parents were still going strong. But this, this hit pretty close to home, and mortality—especially his own—was a subject he had given a lot of thought to during the drive into town. But scared or not, he was glad he'd obeyed the inner voice that had told him he should be there for his dad, that it was the right, adult thing to do.

The woman at the emergency-room desk offered little information beyond the fact that Mrs. Robichaux had been taken into surgery. The news didn't surprise him. All it had taken was one look into Shiloh's eyes to know that she'd gotten a glimpse of the grim reaper. Guilt for the way he'd treated her—and his dad—settled on Jared's shoulders like the weight of the world. How could he have been such a jerk?

While he didn't imagine for a minute that his father had been celibate since the divorce, he'd never flaunted his affairs, never subjected him and Sunny to a string of meaningless women. Whatever he'd done had been done quietly, privately, which is why Shiloh had been such a shock. It had happened so fast, and it was so public. Then, when she'd first told them the truth, it had been hard to imagine that his dad would marry someone just to help them out of a bad spot. But the more he thought about it, the more it made sense. It was exactly the sort of thing Cade Robichaux would do.

Shiloh had never pushed herself off on him and Sunny, either before or since the wedding. She was pleasant, helpful and seemed to want no more than she'd claimed...to be their friend. Actually, she seemed pretty nice, and despite their differences, his dad was a decent guy.

It occurred to Jared again that Cade must have been lonely all these years. Now that he and Sunny were growing up, his dad would be more alone than ever. Maybe he'd married Shiloh not only to help her, but for himself, to infuse his life with some pleasure. Maybe he liked the idea of having a family around him again. After all, he'd missed a lot of his and Sunny's growing up.

Because of the divorce, they'd all missed a lot. Because of the divorce, Jared fought almost daily battles with his feelings. He had been so torn all these years—never spending enough time with his dad to get to know him, liking the heck out of his mom's husband and plagued with guilt because he had more in common with Michael than he did with his real dad.

Blinking back the tears that stung his eyes, Jared made himself a promise—that he'd do the best he could to stick out *his* marriage so his kids wouldn't have to go through the hell called divorce. A sudden thought struck him. Would Shiloh and his dad get a divorce if something happened to her baby?

Jared suddenly, instinctively knew where his father was. His heart was a leaden weight in his chest as he turned the knob of the chapel door. He had no idea what to say to Cade, but he knew he had to open the door, knew he had to be there for him.

His dad lifted his head at the sound of the door opening. Jared's heart slammed against his ribs in an anguished cadence. Cade had been crying. *Crying.* Tears still glistened in his eyes. Without stopping to wonder how he knew, Jared realized that whatever reasons were behind his dad's offer to marry Shiloh, somewhere along the way he'd grown to love her. With the new, adult perception that had guided him through the past hour, he understood that only loving someone could make a person hurt so badly. Holding on to the sides of the pews for support, he made his way closer.

"She didn't . . . die, did she?"

Cade shook his head, and Jared sank down next to him.

"She lost the baby," Cade told him. "It was growing in the fallopian tube instead of the womb, and the tube ruptured. They had to take her into surgery to get the internal bleeding stopped."

Internal bleeding? Fear caused Jared's heart to race. "She's going to be all right, isn't she?"

Cade blew out an unsteady breath. "I hope so. I pray she will be. Ted's a damn fine doctor, but she's been in pain for so long that I worry that she isn't . . . strong enough." Cade's voice broke, and his eyes filled again.

Jared swallowed the massive lump of emotion lodged in his own throat. "I'm sorry, Dad."

Cade looked up sharply.

"I'm sorry I've been so terrible to you and her."

Cade threw his arm around Jared's shoulders and pulled him into a tight embrace. The fact that he couldn't remember the last time he and his son had shared that kind of closeness only added to his sorrow.

"I'm sorry, too," he admitted. "Sorry I wasn't a better father. Sorry I didn't make more of an effort to spend time with you and Sunny."

The twin confessions crumbled the wall that had separated them. Encouraged by Jared's admission,

Cade accepted his part in his failed marriage but tried to explain the circumstances of his youth, hoping Jared could see why he'd been so driven. He also explained that the reason he'd been so hard on Jared lately was that it had occurred to him one day that he'd given him and Sunny too many things, to try to make up for not knowing them.

"This thing with Shiloh brought things to a head. I knew it had to stop. That's why I pressed so hard for you to get a job and take on some responsibility. I love you too much to sit back and watch you turn into a spoiled rich kid."

Jared's nod said he understood. Then it was his turn to explain how torn he'd felt, that his smart mouth had been more than the usual teenage rebellion. "I don't know," he said at last, "I think I figured out that when I was obnoxious I had your undivided attention."

"And that was better than no attention, huh?"

Jared nodded. Silence filled the small room, but it was a comfortable silence. A silence filled with promise. "So what now?" he asked.

"We go on from here. We can't go back and undo the past, but we can learn from our mistakes. We can start over and try to do better from here on out. I'm willing to try if you are."

Jared nodded. "I'm willing."

There was a soft rap at the door before it opened a crack and a nurse stuck her head in. "Mr. Robichaux? Your wife is out of surgery. Dr. Devane will be out to talk to you in a minute."

Cade nodded. "Is she okay?"

"Dr. Devane thinks she'll be fine," the nurse said with a smile. "She's in ICU so we can keep a sharp eye on her, but everything looks good."

"Thank you." *Thank God.*

The woman disappeared, and Cade and Jared exchanged smiles of relief.

"Do you think they'll let you see her?" Jared asked.

"Probably not until she gets out of intensive care. I think I'll stay the night...just in case she...needs anything. There's nothing you can do, son. Why don't you go on home?"

Jared nodded. He rose and started for the door.

"Jared."

He turned.

"Your coming here means more to me than you can imagine."

A hot blush stained Jared's face. His heart sung with pleasure. "No problem."

"Be careful driving home."

"I will."

A few minutes later Ted Devane was shaking Cade's proffered hand. "She came through the surgery like a champ."

"Thank God."

"I don't know if anyone did much explaining to you, or if it all happened so fast you're still in the dark."

"I know it was an ectopic pregnancy."

"Right," he said with a nod. "They're doomed from the start. For some reason the egg lodges in the tube and as the baby grows the pain increases until the tube ruptures, usually by three months. I feel really bad about this, Cade. After seeing her that one time I suspected she might be a candidate for a spontaneous abortion. Eggs that don't develop right happen fairly frequently, and nature has a way of taking care of those situations. But I never had reason from that one visit to suspect an ectopic pregnancy. Knowing her situation, I thought that at least part of her problems were stress related."

Cade nodded. "She certainly had her share of that."

"There is good news, though," Ted said.

"What's that?"

"Shiloh can still have children. It will be harder to conceive, but I see no reason she can't deliver a perfectly healthy baby."

"Come on, Ted, you know our situation. The whole town does."

"Yeah, but things change, old buddy."

Yeah, things changed. And fast. Tonight had showed him that. But would they change enough that Shiloh would want to have a baby with him? Cade wondered. All he could do was take one day at a time. "How soon before she can go home?"

"If things go as well as we expect, four or five days." Ted slapped him on the shoulder. "I'm going to check on her again and head home. How about you?"

"I think I'll stick around . . . at least until I can see her."

Instructed to stay only four or five minutes, Cade opened the door to Shiloh's room. Two IV's dripped life-giving fluids into her body; a monitor blipped with every beat of her heart. She looked so small, even in the twin-size bed. Small and so pale.

Trepidation filled him as he drew nearer. What would he say to her when she awoke? How could he tell her? And how would the news affect their strange alliance? Reaching out a hand, he brushed his thumb along the delicate sweep of her cheekbone. She stirred beneath his touch and her eyes fluttered open.

"Cade." She licked her dry lips.

"Hi. Want some ice?"

"Please."

He gave her a spoonful of ice, and she closed her eyes again. She didn't say anything for so long that he thought she'd drifted off into her medicinal dreams again. Then she asked the question he'd been dreading, the one he'd expected to come later, when she was more awake, more able to understand.

"My baby... What happened to my baby?" She opened her drug-glazed eyes and looked up at him.

A sigh trickled from Cade's own dry lips. His eyes burned with tears. "Ted couldn't save the baby, *chère,*" he said, the admission painful to think, much less say.

He didn't know what he expected from her. Tears, surely, maybe even hysterics. But instead of the tearful, emotional scene he'd envisioned, Shiloh only closed her eyes and murmured, "It's probably better this way."

By the middle of the afternoon Shiloh was lucid enough to realize that she'd had some sort of surgery. Her abdomen burned with a searing agony. It hurt when she moved, hurt when she coughed. She had a vague recollection of Cade saying that she'd lost the baby, and knew that the surgery and pain were connected to that loss.

She welcomed the pain. Deserved it.

Other than despising herself for being so stupid as to be taken in by Jack and berating herself for getting "caught," she'd given little thought to the innocent child she carried in her womb. She'd been so busy worrying about the changes a baby would make in her life and being embarrassed over the gossip, that she hadn't thought of the child growing inside her as an actual entity. She had even defied Cade's orders to call Ted the day following their wedding. At the time it hadn't seemed important. She was feeling better, and as usual, she'd been concerned only with herself, her feelings. She'd never thought that the baby was a real person whose life she would be responsible for shaping, molding.

Scary thought. Terrifying.

She wasn't the nurturing type. She was a career woman. She probably wouldn't have made a good mother, anyway. She must not be too lovable, or she'd have managed to establish a stable, permanent relationship with a man by now. Obviously she wasn't a good judge of people or she wouldn't have fallen for a sleaze like Jack. Add to that the fact that she was selfish and self-centered—her feelings and actions the past couple of months proved that—and the picture of Shiloh Rambler wasn't a pretty one.

No, it was better this way, she told herself again, closing her eyes and trying to block out the picture of despair on Cade's face when he'd told her the news. He would see. They would all see that it was best that the baby never be born rather than have someone like her for a mother.

Unfortunately, settling the matter in her own mind didn't lessen the lesion of hurt festering in her heart.

When Ted came in later that evening and explained that the pregnancy was doomed from the start, she repeated her stance again and again in an effort to stay the pain. She didn't even bat an eye when he told her that he'd had to remove the fallopian tube and that, though she could get pregnant again, it would be harder. She told him that it didn't matter and almost convinced herself she believed it.

The ending of her pregnancy presented another problem: Cade. He'd indicated that part of his willingness to marry her centered on his loneliness and his desire to have a second chance at fatherhood to atone for his mistakes the first time around. But there was no baby now, ergo, no second chance. Would he want to end their marriage, as well? Of course, he said he wanted her, but marriage was certainly not necessary when two consenting adults wanted each other.

Then there was her family to deal with. When Garrett and Molly visited, both dewy-eyed with sorrow, Shiloh listened to their condolences and murmured the appropriate replies. Over the next few days she did her best to smile at their attempts to lift her spirits and accepted their gifts with the correct degree of gratitude and enthusiasm. She chatted with them and even allowed Molly to walk her down the hall in an attempt to build her strength. But she was glad when they left so she no longer had to play the hypocrite.

The truth was that it hurt to look at Molly, who was stunning in the last few weeks of her own pregnancy. She could hardly bear to think of Garrett and Molly's baby, who would no doubt be born the perfect specimen of health. She admitted that she was jealous. She'd once been jealous of her brother's happiness, and now she was jealous of his wife's health and that of their unborn baby. But what else could she expect? Wasn't her jealousy just another mark of her self-indulgence?

Though the pain inside her grew to almost unbearable proportions, she never cried. She'd promised herself weeks ago that she'd shed no more tears over the situation, and it was a promise she intended to keep. Crying was just a sign of weakness. It didn't change things. It hadn't brought back Jack—though that was a blessing in disguise—and it wouldn't bring back their baby. Crying wouldn't change the person she was or her selfish reactions to her prospective motherhood. She might have botched her relationships, perhaps even her whole life, but she damn well didn't intend to be a failure at hiding how much it hurt to know how badly she'd failed.

The sun was shining on Wednesday morning when Cade arrived to take Shiloh home, but he had the feeling that it was raining in her heart.

"Comfortable?" he asked, glancing over at her pale countenance and putting the Bronco in gear.

"I'm fine."

But she wasn't fine. In fact, she was a long way from fine. Though she tried to give the impression that everything was all right, he knew it wasn't. Physically, she gave every appearance of being on the mend; emotionally, everyone was aware that she wasn't dealing with the loss of the baby very well.

She wasn't dealing with it at all.

Cade knew that Ted had told her exactly what had happened, but she refused to discuss the loss or how it was affecting her. If anyone offered a word of commiseration, she was quick to say that things happened for the best and quicker to change the subject. He wasn't a psychoanalyst, but he was smart enough to figure out that Shiloh was in some sort of denial. Even Garrett and Molly agreed that she was depressed.

Ted felt there was some reason that Shiloh was denying herself the healing outlet of grief. Like Cade, he knew she needed to mourn her loss, but his immediate advice was to let nature take its course and pamper her a little. She'd been through a lot the past few months, and time itself had miraculous healing powers. All Cade could do was give Ted's advice a try.

"Molly brought over a casserole for lunch," Cade said in an effort to inject some normalcy into the day.

"That's nice."

"She said it wouldn't be as fancy or as good as what you'd make, but it was the thought that counts."

There was an imperceptible tightening of Shiloh's lips. "On the contrary," she said with a false lightness, "Molly's an excellent cook. In fact, there's nothing Molly doesn't do well."

Cade couldn't say he was surprised by the scarcely veiled venom in her voice. When Garrett and Molly had come to the hospital to visit, he'd noticed that Shiloh could hardly bear to look at her sister-in-law, which only added to his suspicion that Shiloh's acceptance of what had happened was nothing but a brittle facade. She was comparing herself with Molly and coming up short. He was beginning to realize that not only had she not accepted her loss, she had made her inability to carry the baby full term some sort of measuring stick of her self-worth.

Upset about her reaction to the news of losing the baby and uncertain as to what was going on in her mind, Cade had concluded that he could do little but

make her life as easy as possible while she healed—and
pray that that day came fast. The first thing he had
done the morning following her surgery was have
Jared help him put all the antique nursery items back
in the attic. The violet-sprigged bedspread she'd
wanted had been purchased, and the painters had been
instructed to paint the woodwork of the would-be
nursery a forest green as soon as possible, to start the
transformation into a guest room.

He'd thought about hiring some domestic help until Shiloh regained her strength, but when he'd mentioned the idea to Ellen Rambler, she had nixed it.
She'd planned on coming to be there when Molly's
baby was born; she would just come sooner. Shiloh's
mother would be arriving the following day, and Cade
was glad. Maybe Ellen could say or do something to
make Shiloh snap out of the lethargy holding her in its
grip.

"Your mother gets in about ten in the morning," he
offered, hoping to spark some conversational germ.

"I know. You already told me."

"Sorry." Cade felt his already floundering spirits
plummet. Things didn't bode well for a new beginning, at all.

Shiloh insisted on being put in her old bedroom,
even though it meant climbing the stairs. She insisted
that it would be good exercise to help her regain her
strength. Cade acquiesced, even though he would
rather have put her in Jared's room temporarily. By
the time they reached the top, sweat beaded her forehead and her mouth was pinched with strain. He
ached for the pain he knew she must have been feeling, but she insisted she was fine.

Once he got her settled into the tester bed, he went downstairs to warm the casserole for lunch. Shiloh insisted on coming downstairs for the meal, which meant she had to do the stair routine twice more. Cade put his foot down when they'd finished the casserole and salad, insisting that she take a nap. He gave her a pain pill and made her promise that she'd stay in bed while he went out to his office to catch up on a little work. She promised.

She lied.

When he returned to the house three hours later, he was careful to make as little noise as possible, just in case she wasn't awake yet, but when he peeked into her room he saw that the bed was empty. *Shadow Man,* a novel by mystery writer Peggy Milliot, lay on the bedside table, and the radio played softly. A quick look around the room confirmed that she wasn't there. Damn! Why hadn't she stayed put? She was in no shape to go gallivanting around the house when no one was around. Dragging a hand through his hair, Cade turned and left the room.

In the hallway he noticed that the door to the adjoining room, the room that was to have been the nursery, was ajar. Cautiously, not knowing what to expect, he pushed it farther open. Her shoulders back, her spine rigid, Shiloh stood in the center of the emptiness, facing him. Her eyes were as vacant as the room.

Hurt sluiced through him. It was as if she was there in body only, as if her mind had wandered away from her, gone somewhere where pain couldn't find it. Indecision held him rooted to the spot. He had no idea how to reach her, didn't know what to do or say.

"What did you do with the baby things?"

Cade was so surprised to hear her speak, and so lucidly, that the words didn't register for a moment. "What?"

"I asked what you'd done with the baby things you found in the attic."

Relief leeched the starch from his spine, and he leaned against the doorjamb. "Jared and I put them back into the attic," he told her. "I didn't want you to come home and see them and... be sad."

"You could have left them," she said, sharpness in her voice. "The baby is dead, Cade. It's time you accepted that." As quickly as she could, she crossed the room toward the doorway.

The insinuation that she was dealing with the death of the baby and he wasn't kindled more than a little irritation inside him. As she brushed past him, he took her upper arm in a firm but gentle grip. The frustration he'd felt the past few days laced his voice. Frustration and an anger he wasn't even aware he was harboring. "You're the one who needs to do some accepting, *chère*. You're the one who's in denial here."

"I haven't denied anything!" she cried, wrenching her arm free. "I just said it. The baby is dead. Dead!"

"And are you glad about that?"

For a second she just stared at him as if she couldn't believe what he'd just asked. Then her palm struck his cheek in a blow that sent his head reeling to one side.

"How dare you imply that I don't care!"

"If you care, why don't you cry? Why don't you grieve?"

"What will crying change?" she challenged. "And how do you know I'm not grieving? You don't have any idea what's going on inside me. You don't know what it's like to lose a child."

Shame and regret raged through Cade like the waters of the bayou in the spring rains. Damn it! How could he have allowed his anger to get out of control when she was still so fragile in every way?

"Oh, but you're wrong, *chère.*" His voice held an aching tenderness. "I do know. I lost two of them once, remember? And I'm just now figuring out how to get them back."

The gentle reminder stripped Shiloh of her own fury. Her shoulders slumped and her eyelashes drooped to hide her eyes. "I'm tired," she said.

Without a word Cade swept her into his arms and carried her to her room. He eased her onto the bed and pulled the sheet up over her. Satisfied that she was as comfortable as he could make her, he straightened. "Can I get you anything before I start dinner?"

She shook her head. Her short hair was a dark, silken cloud against the pristine whiteness of the pillowcase. Cade went to the doorway and turned, more sorry than he could say for upsetting her. How could he have hurt her like that, when all he wanted to do was take her in his arms and hold her until all the pain went away? What had he been thinking?

That's just it, Robichaux. You weren't thinking. It was true. He'd just reacted to his own pain and lack of understanding. What he really wanted to tell her was that he would be glad to do his part and give her half a dozen babies if that would make her happy. But of course, she wouldn't want that. The baby she'd lost had been conceived in love—at least on her part. A substitute wouldn't be the same at all.

"I'm sorry I flew off the handle," he said, wondering if she would ever forgive him. She only looked at him for a moment, and then she closed her eyes. Cade shut the door behind him and made his way down the stairs. Even though he had only met his mother-in-law once, he could hardly wait for Ellen's arrival.

Shiloh claimed she didn't feel like coming down for dinner, so Cade carried her scrambled eggs and bacon up on a tray. When he returned for the dishes an hour later, he saw that she'd hardly touched the food. She was awake, staring at a place across the room, her eyes half closed, as if she was watching some scene unfold in her mind.

"Finished?"

Her eyes followed him across the room. "Yes."

"I'm sorry. I'm not much of a cook."

Her gaze slid from his. "It wasn't the food. I just wasn't hungry." A sigh trickled from her lips, and she eased to her side. "I'm just very tired." She tucked her hand beneath her cheek and closed her eyes.

Abruptly Cade put down the tray and went to the window, though he couldn't have said what he saw below him. He scraped his hand through his hair.

"We need to talk." Before she could answer, he plunged ahead. "First of all, I'd like to say that I'm sorry for the way I behaved this afternoon. It was uncalled for. You're right. I don't know how you feel, and I have no right to judge you, even if I did."

She didn't answer. He assumed she was thinking about what he'd said.

Cade cleared his throat. "It occurred to me this afternoon that this...changes things between us. I'd never want to stand in the way of your happiness, and I wanted to let you know that if you want your freedom to go back to your old life, I'll be glad to give you an annulment."

Squaring his shoulders, preparing for the blow that would send his world crashing down around him, Cade waited for her to answer. And waited. Finally, when he could bear the suspense no longer, he turned to face her. Shiloh lay nestled in the bed, her upper body rising and falling with the even rhythm of her breathing.

She was asleep.

Cade felt like laughing. He felt like crying. So much for noble gestures, he thought, tiptoeing across the room and picking up her tray. He left her to her sleep and hopefully to her rest.

She should have stayed awake, he thought. He wasn't sure when—if ever—he would get up the courage to offer her her freedom again.

Chapter Eleven

Shiloh kept her eyes closed until she was certain Cade had left the room. She'd feigned sleepiness because she hadn't wanted to talk . . . because she'd had an intuitive feeling she didn't want to hear what he was going to say. She was right. And when he'd offered to set her free of their vows she had pretended to be asleep so he couldn't witness the panic and despair his offer had engendered. Until she was faced with the prospect of losing him, she hadn't been aware of just how much she'd come to rely on his strength.

As usual, his gesture was an unselfish one.

Was it, really? a small, self-pitying voice inside her prompted.

Maybe Cade didn't want to stay married to her because the new status quo didn't suit his own needs. After all, he'd counted on becoming a father to her child, not marrying an emotional cripple.

She didn't know why he had made her the offer. She wasn't sure of much of anything anymore. All she was certain of was that losing Cade after losing the baby was more than she thought she could bear, much harder than losing either Jack or his baby. And it was just one thing more that proved her a failure.

Knowing her true feelings for Cade brought no pleasure. Instead it brought a new surge of guilt and misery. Inevitably, her thoughts turned to Jack.

She wondered what he was doing and who he'd been with while she lay alone in a strange room recovering from the loss of their child. Several times since she'd awakened from the surgery she'd thought of calling to tell him that the baby was history, that he didn't have to worry about being slapped with a paternity suit or having her appear on his doorstep, a little Jack Junior in tow, demanding some sort of financial support.

But no matter how many ways she played the scenario, she knew she wouldn't call. She couldn't bear to contemplate talking to him, couldn't bear to think of him. Thinking of him and the past reminded her of what a fool she had been to believe in him and his slick lies, thoughts that only deepened the depression that showed little sign of abating. Unlike her, Jack hadn't had to worry about any of it. As she suspected he was accustomed to doing, Jack Delaney had gotten off scot-free—no hurts, no scars, no regrets.

Garrett went with Cade to the airport to pick up Shiloh's mother. Cade watched Ellen hug Garrett, then she embraced Cade as if they were old and dear friends. When she drew back to look at him, there were tears in her eyes.

"How is she?"

"Not good," Cade acknowledged. "As far as I know, she hasn't shed a tear. It's like she's...dead inside."

"And before you plan any family get-togethers to cheer her up, you may as well know that she's jealous of Molly," Garrett said.

"Jealous of Molly!" Ellen said. "Why?"

"Because Molly's pregnancy is going so well, and she knows we're probably going to have a healthy baby."

"Does she talk about it?"

Cade shook his head. "No. Not to me, at least."

"She hasn't talked to anyone," Garrett added. "She pretends that everything is okay, that it's no big deal, that what happened is best for everyone."

"Not only will she not talk, she won't take an interest in anything. She's stopped helping on the house. She doesn't even want to talk about decorating. Hell, she won't do anything. She just sits and stares at the four walls!" Cade said in frustration.

"Not a good situation," Ellen said with a worried frown. She sighed. "Well, I'll see if I can get her to open up."

For more than a week, Ellen gave it her best shot. When she and Shiloh sat shelling purple hull peas, she tried to start with a discussion of how the surgery would affect Shiloh's future and work backwards to the baby. Shiloh balked. When they took short walks down the old road that passed the slave quarters, Ellen tried to cajole her daughter into talking...to no avail. Finally, out of ideas and out of sorts, Ellen resorted to telling her daughter that it wasn't healthy to keep her feelings bottled up inside her, but Shiloh only looked at her with those calm blue eyes that reflected nothing of the pain shredding her heart.

Then, ten days after she came home from the hospital, two short weeks after losing Jack's baby, the inevitable happened. Cade, Shiloh and Ellen were sitting on the sleeping porch— Cade and Ellen talking about an item they'd seen on the evening news, Shiloh just sitting, mesmerized by the sluggishly moving bayou— when the phone rang.

"I'll get it," Cade said, relieved at the thought of a moment's respite from watching Shiloh's withdrawal from the world. He took the call in the wide hallway that divided the lower floor of the house in half. "Magnolia Manor."

"Cade. It's Garrett. Molly's gone into labor, and I wondered if you could come and get Laura Leigh."

In spite of himself Cade felt a twinge of something close to jealousy himself. He squashed it immediately. "Sure. Is Molly okay?"

Garrett laughed. "She's walking the floor and giving orders like a drill sergeant."

"Good," Cade said, a smile curving his lips at the picture that came to mind. "Tell her I'll be right there." He hung up and went back out onto the porch. "Molly's gone into labor," he said without preamble. "Garrett wants me to bring Laura Leigh over here."

"Is Molly all right?" Ellen asked.

"She's fine."

Ellen rose. "Let me get my purse, and I'll ride with you."

"Why don't you just go ahead and take your things over there?" Shiloh said, making her first contribution to a conversation in almost an hour.

Both Ellen and Cade looked at her. Her face was devoid of color, and there was a look in her eyes that Cade couldn't quite define.

Ellen cast Cade a wry smile. "If I didn't know better, I'd think she was tryin' to get rid of me."

"Of course I'm not trying to get rid of you." Annoyance sharpened Shiloh's voice. "I just thought it might be easier on you and Laura Leigh if she's in a familiar environment. I'm well enough to take care of myself now."

Ellen looked doubtful. "I'm not so sure about that, and I don't have my things together. I think we'll bring Laura over here, at least for tonight. We can rethink things tomorrow."

Shiloh shrugged. Her look of insouciance encompassed them both. "Fine."

"We won't be gone long," Cade told her.

Ellen went to her daughter and dropped a kiss to her forehead. "Don't go chasin' around the yard while we're gone, now, hear?" she teased.

"I'll be fine."

There was no denying Shiloh's irritation. Cade and Ellen exchanged concerned looks as they left her sitting there in the gathering twilight and her misery.

Shiloh didn't want to see Laura Leigh. She wasn't sure how she would react to the child, who would only serve to remind her of what she'd lost. Unlike Cade and her mother, the lovely Laura Leigh wouldn't understand that her silence meant she didn't want to talk. She'd keep at a person until they were forced to respond...and Shiloh wasn't sure she could interact with her niece on any level without stirring up the pain that lay dormant and festering inside her very soul. She chewed on her bottom lip and let the day draw to a close around her.

They weren't gone long. She heard them come in, all three of them chattering and laughing and acting as if everything was all right in their worlds. For a fraction of a second Shiloh wished she could join them, but she banished the thought. She'd already pushed aside her baby's needs for her own selfish wishes; the least she could do was hold on to her sorrow.

Still, she wasn't prepared for Laura Leigh's particular brand of seduction. The child barreled onto the sleeping porch but skidded to a stop a few feet away.

"Turn on lights," she commanded.

"Good idea," Cade said, doing just that.

Shiloh blinked in the sudden brightness and looked up at her husband, who was standing in the doorway, a look of concern on his rugged face. "I didn't realize it was so dark," she said.

Laura stood before her, her hands clasped behind her back, a puzzled expression in her eyes, her red-gold hair billowing out around her pert face like a fiery cloud. A giant hand squeezed Shiloh's heart. Fresh pain snatched her breath. The child was so incredibly beautiful.

"You got a bo-bo?" Laura asked with solemn concern.

The empathy coming from such an unexpected source undermined Shiloh's defenses. She swallowed the sudden lump of emotion that clotted in her throat. "Yes."

"Where?"

How could she respond to such innocent curiosity with anything less than complete honesty? Shiloh touched her abdomen. "Here—" Her voice cracked, and she moved her hand over her heart "—and here."

"Kisses make it all better."

Dear God... "Kisses never hurt," she agreed in a quavering voice.

Smiling, Laura held out her arms and went to Shiloh, who had no recourse but to lean forward and take the child into a loose embrace. Laura gave her a grunting, big-as-the-world hug and a wet, smacking kiss on the cheek. Shiloh's heart felt full to overflowing. The genuine concern that radiated from the child chipped a crack in the shell of bitterness and self-loathing that had held her captive for two long weeks.

She couldn't let that happen. She owed it to her baby to suffer. Without a word she loosened Laura's hold on her neck and stood, wanting nothing but to get away from the feelings threatening to swamp her. *Needing* to get away. Trembling from head to toe, she started across the porch. Cade still stood near the doorway, regarding her with an expression of sorrow.

She'd forgotten he was there. Hoping he wouldn't stop her, she brushed past him into the hallway where she almost collided with her mother, who was carrying a tray of milk and cookies.

"What's the matter?" Ellen asked, her voice sharp with concern.

Shiloh was too intent on escaping the threatening tumult of emotions to answer.

"Shiloh, you've got to go with us," Ellen said. "You've really hurt Molly's and Garrett's feelings.

They're starting to think you just don't care a fig about Rett.''

It was a variation of the same tune Shiloh had heard ever since Molly had been delivered of a nine-pound-one-ounce boy two days before. Ever since she'd fled the screened porch and the feelings Laura Leigh's concern had elicited inside her, Shiloh had been eaten up with guilt for her inability to rush to her sister-in-law's side and lavish her with good wishes.

She was happy for Molly and Garrett. Truly. She was almost sick with relief that things had gone well for Molly and baby Rett, who, like all first-born Rambler males had been named Jonathan Garrett Rambler. Shiloh just wasn't sure she could say those things without flying into a million pieces.

Crossing her arms over her breasts as if she was protecting herself against that fear, she rose and began to pace the room. "Of course I care," she argued a bit testily.

"Then go and see your nephew." Ellen rose and went to her daughter, putting her hands on Shiloh's rigid shoulders. "I know it will be hard for you, honey. It will be agony. I know you're happy for your brother, but at the same time, you're probably askin' yourself—why me? Why not them?"

A small gasp of surprise escaped Shiloh's lips. "How did you know?"

"Because you're human, and no matter how good a person we are, those uncharitable thoughts creep in—just for a moment—and make us feel like the lowest form of humanity for thinkin' them. Am I right?"

Shiloh nodded.

"Unless you're an absolute saint, those are normal feelings, honey. But I know, and you know, that you don't mean them. I know you're happy for Molly and Garrett and that you'd never wish anythin' bad for their baby."

Her mother's understanding was having the same effect on her that Laura's concern had: it undermined her self-imposed martyrdom. The eyes that met Ellen's steady, compassionate gaze were filled with remorse.

"No," Shiloh said in a harsh whisper. "I wouldn't really wish anything bad for them."

"The baby is your nephew. You'll have to face him and Molly sooner or later. The first time will be the hardest."

"I know." There was agony in her eyes.

"Will you go with Cade to the hospital?"

Shiloh's eyelashes drifted shut, as if she prayed for guidance. The stiffness left her body. "I'll go."

Shiloh was in torment. So far she had made the short trip to Thibodaux General in stony silence. The only sound in the car was the tortured squeaking of leather as she mutilated the shoulder strap of her purse between her twisting fingers. There was dread in the stiff set of her shoulders. Pain in the shadows haunting her eyes. Tension in the pinched tightness of her lips.

She'd lost weight, and Cade could have sworn that there was a sprinkling of white hair in her temples that hadn't been there when she'd first come from Tennessee. For the first time since he'd known her, and despite the splashes of color on her cheeks and lips, she looked every bit of her thirty-four years.

He wished he could say or do something to help, but she shut him out at every turn. Cut him off with a look. Blocked him out by turning away. He didn't know what course to take next; neither did Ellen.

Cade guided the car into the hospital parking lot, turned off the engine and glanced over at Shiloh, who was as pale as death. Without a word he got out and rounded the hood to her side of the car, swinging the passenger door wide. She just sat there, unwilling—or unable—to move. Pain and compassion filled his heart. God only knew what she must be feeling. But like Ellen, Cade knew that this was a step Shiloh not only needed to take, but had to take.

Resting his left forearm on the top of the car, he leaned forward and extended his hand, palm up. She looked at the hand for a moment and then tilted back her head to look at him with anguished eyes. The message in his eyes told her that she could do it. A sigh shuddered through her. He watched her visibly square her shoulders before placing her hand in his.

Molly looked bright and chipper and beautiful. It hurt to look at her, but Shiloh faced her sister-in-law's happiness with more bravery than she'd known she had. If it hadn't been for Cade, she couldn't have done it. She thought of the moment when he'd helped her from the car and his fingers had closed warmly around hers. She'd accepted his offering of comfort the way a drowning man latches onto a lifeline. Instead of releasing his hold on her hand when she was out of the car, he had laced his fingers through hers, and their clasped hands had swung between them as they made their way to the entrance.

She hadn't pulled away. It had crossed her mind that he was the only thing holding her up, that his stability and strength were all she had. She was marginally aware that she'd gripped his fingers tighter. If she lost that, if she lost him . . .

"Well, are you ready to go see the baby?" Garrett asked, breaking into her troubled thoughts with the suggestion she'd been dreading. Cade glanced over at her, and the look in his eyes seemed to ask if she could handle it. She forced a smile to her lips and took a deep breath.

"Sure," she said with a shrug. "Let's go see the baby."

Refusing Cade's hand—she had to do this part alone—she followed the trio down the hall to the nursery window where the newborns were lined up like wares for sale. Shiloh stood well back from the window, gathering her meager courage while they laughed and oohed and aahed and talked about who baby Rett looked like. Her heart was beating fast, and each breath that passed her lips was shallow, hardly sufficient to keep her alive. A wave of dizziness washed over her, and a suffocating blackness gathered before her eyes. Was she going to pass out and make a complete fool of herself?

"What do you think, Shiloh?"

The question, though she had no idea what they were asking, jolted her back to the immediate problem. She took a firm grip on her emotions and stepped closer. Though she still felt light-headed, the darkness had abated. "What?"

"Who do you think he looks like?" Molly asked, pride glowing in her eyes.

Molly and Cade stepped aside, making a place for her. Other than outright refusal, there was nothing she could do but look at her nephew. She felt as if she were moving in slow motion as she put one foot in front of the other. When she reached the window she felt Cade's arm go around her shoulders and draw her to his side. She was glad for the support. Drawing in a deep, fortifying breath, she braced herself for her first look at the baby.

He was tiny, she thought with surprise. He looked so small... even at nine pounds. He was wrapped tightly in a receiving blanket and was sleeping, his knees drawn up under him, his little bottom sticking up in the air. His hair, as dark as Garrett's, was long and thick. He looked like Garrett, she thought. He looked like his daddy. Regret, sharp and piercing, knifed through her.

His tiny hand twitched. A longing so poignant that it bordered on pain snatched her breath, and without realizing what she was doing she raised both hands to the window, as if the action could bring her closer to the child asleep in its sterile crib. Though there was no pacifier in sight, his little bow-shaped mouth moved in a sucking motion that pulled without mercy on Shiloh's heartstrings.

She clamped her trembling lips together and pressed her palms to the glass. She would never see her son sleeping. Never feel the softness of his skin or see those baby hands reaching for her. She would never feel the tug of his lips on her breast or see them shape those first faltering words.

Shiloh was so wrapped up in her loss that she didn't see it coming. A low wail, rooted in the very heart of her psyche, escaped her compressed lips, and the tears she'd refused to let fall filled her eyes and ran unchecked down her cheeks. Her grief, more intense because it had been repudiated for so long, would not be denied a second more.

She felt Cade's arms go around her from behind and turned in his embrace, locking her arms around him. She wasn't aware that Molly and Garrett were looking at her as if she'd finally stepped across that imaginary line into the world of insanity. Sobs racked her slender body, but now that they had been allowed their way, there was no stopping the torrent of tears. Holding on to Cade as if she would never let him go, she looked up at him through a veil of moisture.

"My baby was a boy, too, Cade," she choked out around the harsh, ugly sobs that tore at her throat. "Ted said that he was a perfect little boy."

The confession took the last of her strength. She collapsed against him.

"Is everything all right?" The concerned query came from a nurse who, seeing the unfolding scene, had stepped out of the nursery.

"Everything's fine," she heard Cade say as he pressed her face against him and rocked her back and forth.

Dear God, she hoped he was right.

The waiting room down the hallway from the nursery was empty except for Shiloh and Cade, who was thankful that she'd been able to cry out her misery in private. Knowing that all he could do was offer her a shoulder and his support, that's exactly what he'd done. She'd cried for a long time. For aeons. Harshly. So long he'd begun to worry that maybe too many tears were as bad as too few . . . or none. But she had stopped at last and had drawn free of his arms, reality and acceptance replacing her misery.

She mopped at her eyes with a handful of tissues she'd taken from her purse, and then she wadded them into a tight ball. She kept her gaze focused on her task. "I'm sorry." Like her hands, her voice trembled.

Cade, who was sitting next to her, stilled her hands with one of his. "For what?"

She looked up at him with red and swollen eyes. Mascara streaked her cheeks. She looked down at her hands and swapped her wadding technique for a shredding method. "For going to pieces like that. For embarrassing you and Molly and Garrett." She gave a short, shaky laugh. "Those nurses probably thought I was a basket case."

The moment she spoke the words her gaze flew to his and her teeth clamped down on her bottom lip. She knew, he thought. She knew that her actions the past couple of weeks hadn't been those of a mentally healthy person.

"On the contrary," he told her in a gentle voice, "I think your crying may have kept you from becoming a basket case."

Her eyes filled with tears again, and she nodded in agreement.

"Talk to me *chère*," he urged, taking a tight hold on both her hands. "Tell me how you felt when you lost the baby. Get it out so you can start to heal."

She stared into his eyes for long moments, as if she were weighing her options, or trying to decide if she could trust him with the truth. "Guilty," she said at last. "I felt guilty."

He hadn't expected that. "For God's sake, why?"

She drew in a deep, fortifying breath. "Because until I came here and you offered to marry me, I was ambivalent about how I felt about having a baby." She gave her head an emphatic shake. "No. That isn't true. I'm not sure I ever thought about it as a baby. I thought about it as a mistake. A mistake I was ashamed of. I never considered what kind of mother I'd be. All I could think of was how my life was changed, ruined."

Cade felt it was more important to listen than to comment.

She brushed at her leaking eyes. "The whole thing seemed almost—" she gave a halfhearted shrug "—surreal. I never felt movement. I'm not sure that I ever came to terms with the fact that it was a child I carried inside me. The only thing that *was* real was the sickness and the pain."

She looked up at Cade. "Maybe that's why God took the baby—to punish me for not caring enough."

"God wasn't punishing you when you lost the baby. It was just one of those things that happen. No one knows why. It's wrong for you to blame yourself, wrong for you to think you deserved what you got— that is what you thought, isn't it?"

She nodded.

"Well, stop it. Under the circumstances, your feelings were normal."

"I'd like to believe that."

"Do believe it. You were dealing with a whole set of problems you'd never confronted before. I think that your uncertainty, your resentment, even your rejection of the whole thing were perfectly acceptable responses. You were hurt and insecure over the way Jack had treated you, and blaming yourself for being a bad judge of character. You took all the blame. But I know you. I've watched you with Laura Leigh. If you hadn't had that miscarriage, you'd have come to love the idea of having a child in your life. And you'd have made a wonderful mother."

The flickering hope in her eyes told him that she wanted to believe him. Needed to. "Thank you," she said again, giving his hands a tight squeeze.

"For what?" he repeated.

"For listening." Her voice broke. "For caring."

Cade's slow smile was like the sun breaking through the clouds after a summer thunderstorm. "That's what husbands do, *chère.*"

Chapter Twelve

The cry and the talk with Cade acted as a catharsis. Shiloh, as well as those around her, sensed an immediate change in her attitude and her physical improvement. Her smile came more often; her appetite picked up. But in her own eyes the most marked sign of improvement was her ability to visit the new baby without anything but an occasional twinge of the old pain to haunt her. She was able to play the role of doting aunt and play it honestly. As her guilt and remorse diminished with the passing of each sultry summer day, she knew she was healing.

It was amazing how soon she'd begun to think of Magnolia Manor as home and to expect Sunny and Jared to pop in at all hours. Shiloh still considered the day they'd planned Sunny's party to be the day things began to change between them. Her friendship with Cade's daughter grew daily. Even when she had been the most depressed and unlovable, Sunny had called every day to see how she was doing.

Though Jared had slept at the house when she'd first come home from the hospital, he had stayed away most of the daylight hours, probably so he wouldn't have to face her. Considering her state of mind, she couldn't blame him. It was a wonder she hadn't run everyone off.

But lately he had started hanging around more and talking to her. When he'd expressed his sorrow about the baby, he'd looked as if he was about to burst into tears. And when he asked her to help him pick out a birthday present and bake a cake for his new girl-friend, Shiloh knew their relationship had crossed some imaginary line and that things between them could only improve from there.

As her scars faded and her health and self-esteem reestablished their roots, Shiloh faced a new problem: Cade. They had never discussed where their relationship was headed, and the memory of his offer to let her go echoed through her mind like a melancholy refrain from an old, scratched record with a needle stuck in the groove.

How could she make it without him? Though she'd witnessed his temper, his patience was almost unending, his strength the only constant in her life. The thought of leaving was…unthinkable. The idea of not sitting across the table from him while he ate his breakfast and grumbled about having to get up so early was heartbreaking. The possibility that she'd never know what it was like to lie naked in his arms was unbearable.

She found herself wishing things could be different between them and wondering why fate played such unfair tricks on people. She'd known Cade half her life. Why had it taken the affair with Jack to bring them together? Why had she never come into contact with him when she'd visited Molly and Garrett before?

She sighed. Asking herself why wouldn't change things. She was tired of living with fear of failure. Tired of being afraid to make a mistake. As careful as she'd been, she'd *still* made a big mistake by falling for Jack. She was sick of accepting what life tossed her way. If she wanted happiness, she'd have to go out and find it herself. It wasn't going to come to her.

Actually, her happiness was right there...within arm's reach, if only she could figure out how to latch onto it. Cade would make her happy. Living with him and loving him until they were both old and gray would make her happy. Having his baby would make her ecstatic.

Could she make those dreams come true? He'd said that he wanted their marriage to be a real one after she was over Jack, but wanting sex didn't mean he would want a family. Did he really want to start all over again with sleepless nights and dirty diapers? And how would she approach him about it? If she went to him and told him that she loved him and wanted their marriage to be a real one, would he believe her? He'd made no secret of wanting her before they married, but she'd been so...negative after she'd lost the baby that maybe she'd turned his desire into loathing.

She spent the month following her confession of her guilt watching and waiting as Cade helped with the outside work around the plantation and oversaw the finishing touches on the house, searching for some sign that his interest in her was still there.

Sometimes it seemed that his slow smile or his actions were specifically designed to make her aware of him. She watched him load hay onto the flatbed trailer and shivered with delight as perspiration matted the hair on his chest and trailed down his flat brown abdomen in a salty trail. She dreamed of kissing the runnels of liquid away, of dipping her tongue into the indention of his navel, of stripping away his sweat-stained jeans and exploring his hard, masculine body to her heart's content.

He was driving her crazy.

The day Ted Devane gave her a clean bill of health Shiloh drew a sigh of relief. The past was truly behind her now. Her future lay ahead. It was up to her to make it the best it could be.

She was almost embarrassed to do so, but she stopped by Rambler's Rest and falteringly mentioned her plight to Molly. Her sister-in-law just smiled and offered her some sage advice. "If you want him, seduce him."

"What if he doesn't want me? What if he turns me down?"

Molly only looked at her with eyebrows lifted in disbelieving arches. "The man is crazy about you. Do us all a favor and put him out of his misery."

Shiloh was still wondering how to start a seduction that evening when Cade came home. She was in the room that was to have been the nursery, thinking of the past and pondering the future, when she heard him call her name.

"I'm in here!"

He appeared in the doorway, twin slashes of concern etched between his eyebrows. "Are you all right?"

Shiloh knew that he was wondering if she was having some sort of relapse. "I'm fine. I just came in here to measure for the curtains."

"Oh. I thought—"

"You thought I was brooding over the past."

He shifted his weight to one booted foot and scraped a hand through his hair. "Yeah."

Shiloh crossed the room to stand in front of him. "I'm not brooding. I'm celebrating."

"Celebrating?"

She nodded. "Ted says I'm fine—great, in fact. He said that I can resume all...normal activities." She paused then plunged ahead before she lost her courage. "I'd like to start tonight."

Cade looked at her, a question in his eyes.

Shiloh placed her palms against his chest. The muscles beneath her fingertips grew taut. "I've tried all day to think of something to do or say that might be tantalizing or sexy, but I can't think of anything that doesn't seem phony. The only thing that works for me is to just say it."

"Say what?" he asked, but she could see by the look on his face that he had a pretty good idea what was coming. The expectant tenderness in his eyes gave her the courage to say the words.

"I want you." She felt his hands clamp onto her waist. "And if you still want me, I'm ready for this to be a real marriage."

"Want you?" he rasped. "I want you so much it hurts to look at you."

Shiloh slid her palms up over the firm muscles of his shoulders. "Show me," she breathed on a sigh.

His hands moved down to cup her bottom, drawing her against the hardness of his thighs. His head lowered and his lips grazed hers. Once. Twice. Three times. Emotion tangled in her throat at the sweet reverence in his kisses.

"You taste so good," he breathed against her ear. His hands ranged over the swell of her buttocks and up to cup her breasts. "And sweet heaven, you feel so good."

Shiloh moved her hands between them and worked a button free of its mooring. "So do you." Another fastening fell prey to her nimble fingers. And another. Grasping his shirtfront, she tugged it from his jeans.

His hands took hers captive. "Are you sure this is what you want?" he asked. "Are you sure there are no more ghosts? Because if I ever get you out of those clothes, there's no turning back."

Love light gleamed in Shiloh's eyes. She couldn't tell him that what she felt for him far outweighed the feelings she'd had for Jack. She couldn't say the words, not until she was sure of how he felt. But she could show him. "I'm positive."

Cade released her hands and moved his to either side of her head, threading his fingers through the short glistening strands of her hair. He tilted her head back until their eyes met. "God, I love your hair. It's so sexy."

She smiled. "Most men like long hair."

"So sue me."

He stopped any comment she might have made with a slow, wet kiss that stole her breath. She felt her body go limp and leaned into his strength. With a soft sigh of surrender, she wrapped her arms around his lean middle and pressed her lower body to his.

Taking the sigh for the acquiescence it was, Cade's mouth ranged over her face in a series of open-mouthed kisses. She felt his teeth take her chin in a love bite and felt the tip of his tongue as he trailed a string of sizzling kisses down the arch of her neck. When she realized that he was unfastening the tiny buttons that held the front of her dress together, a shiver of delight quivered through her.

Using his mouth to nudge aside the shoulder of the scoop-necked, floral-patterned dress, he kissed his way down her collarbone. Angling her head to accommo-date him, she freed the last button of his shirt, want-ing, needing to feel the heat of his skin against hers.

It was warm, and the bramble of chest hair that sprawled over his pectoral muscles and down his washboard belly curled crisply against her palms. She leaned forward, burying her face in the cloud of dark hair and breathing in the heady masculine scent of him. Cade drew in a harsh breath near her ear.

Encouraged by his response, she let her mouth search out one flat masculine nipple, circling it with the tip of her tongue. Cade, who was busy with the rest of her buttons, gave a low groan.

"You got an hour to stop that, *chère,*" he said into her ear. The husky passion in his voice accentuated his Cajun accent.

While her fingers were busy with the fastening of his jeans, he stripped the dress from her arms. It fell around her ankles in a bright puddle of color. She felt the front catch of her bra give, felt her breasts spring free of their lacy confines only to be recaptured by the warmth of his hands. He plumped the mounds of soft flesh upward, and his thumbs worried her nipples to aching hardness.

When he bent and took one sensitive tip into the warm wetness of his mouth, suckling on it with a tender tugging of tongue and lips, she felt the response in the very core of her femininity.

Cade's mouth, rougher now with his growing passion, roamed at will over her—her neck, her shoulders, her breasts. She arched her back to give his marauding mouth access to her tingling flesh and surged against him, trying to get as close as possible with the barriers of his jeans and her panties still between them . . . pressing close, rubbing her lower body against his denim-clad thigh in an ancient rhythm that fanned the embers of her need . . . and his.

It wasn't enough. She wanted to *feel* him. His hardness. His heat. Aching to get closer still, she kicked free of her dress and freed the metal fastener of his Wranglers. Catching the corner of her lower lip with her teeth, she scraped her nails lightly down his abdomen to the barrier of his snug-fitting jeans.

Cade sucked in his breath, giving her questing fingers access, and ample room for maneuvers. When she touched him, he stilled, uttering a curse. She wasn't even sure he was breathing. Looking up at him in question, she saw that his eyes were hazy with desire. He wanted her. He really wanted her. Heady exultation raced through her.

Keeping her gaze locked with his, she freed one hand and unzipped his jeans while the other worked its brand of magic. When the zipper reached its lowest point, Cade took her hands in his and pressed moist kisses to her palms and the tiny pulse racing in her wrists. Easing her hands from his, she slipped out of her panties, sending them the way of her dress. She stood before him, hoping that what he saw was pleasing, hoping that she wouldn't disappoint him. Hoping...

Cade started to shimmy out of his jeans.

"Let me."

Her voice sounded too loud in the silence of the room. Even the song of the whippoorwill outside the open French doors sounded as if it called from the far side of tomorrow.

Loving the feel of his hair-dusted thighs against her hands, she pushed the Wranglers and his briefs downward. Trying to keep her gaze averted from the blatant sight of his arousal, she dropped to her knees and peeled off one sock and then the other. Slowly, making a sensual production of the act, caressing his calves, pressing kisses to his thighs, she eased his legs from the confining denim and started kissing her way up the long length of them.

When she reached midthigh, he gave a low growl of need and, taking her bare shoulders into his hands, lifted her to her feet and drew her against him, capturing her mouth in a hot, wet kiss. His tongue plundered the warm receptacle of her mouth while his fingers invaded the moist cavern of her femininity, seeking out the tiny point of pleasure and threatening to destroy her by kindling a searing passion that spread through her like a brush fire.

Senses sang. Nerve endings crackled with the electricity generated by his touch. There was nothing in her world but the sound of Cade's breathing, the touch of his hands, the feel and taste of his flesh. She was lost...to everything but his touch and the feelings building inside her. And the beauty of it was that she didn't care. Couldn't worry about what might happen tomorrow. There was no room for worry...no time....

Hooking an arm around her, Cade lifted her up his body. Parting her legs to encircle his lean torso he guided her onto the throbbing shaft of his manhood. Shiloh gasped, a sound he mistook for pain.

"I'm sorry," he murmured against her shoulder. His voice was filled with anguish, regret. "I didn't mean to hurt you."

"It doesn't hurt," she contradicted, shifting so that he filled her even deeper. "It's good...so very good."

The words were all the encouragement he needed. He managed to move the few steps to the wall, pressing her against it, pressing himself into her body as if he wanted to imprint her with the mark of his possession, branding her with his need, filling her aching emptiness as he erased every old pain, and blotted out every scar from her heart and her womb with the showering of his love.

"It must have worked," Molly said the following afternoon, as she added a dollop of horseradish to the coleslaw dressing.

Shiloh, who was slicing cucumbers for a vegetable tray to accompany their Sunday-afternoon barbecue, looked up from her chore, her face aflame. "What do you mean?"

Molly rolled her eyes. " 'What do you mean?' the lady says. I mean that you must have taken my advice about seducing your husband."

Shiloh couldn't have stopped the sappy grin from curving her lips if she'd known she was going to be drawn and quartered for it. She and Cade had made love for hours. Hours. In bed and out. Against the wall. In the rocker. On the violet-sprinkled bed-spread. "Does it show?"

"Show? Other than noticing that the man sud-denly can't keep his eyes or his hands off you and the fact that you've got indisputable whisker burn on your shoulder, nah, it doesn't show at all."

Shiloh's eyes smiled but her voice was serious. "He's wonderful, Molly."

"I'm glad for you. You deserve wonderful."

Shiloh's smile moved to her mouth. "Yeah, I do, don't I?"

The midafternoon meal was over except for the requisite moanings and groanings about eating too much. Sunny and Jared and their friends had aban-doned the adults for a new movie that was showing. Shiloh was rocking a fussy Rett to sleep, and Molly and Garrett—squashed in the lounge chair together— were making desultory conversation with Cade, who was sprawled in the other lounge chair, when they heard the pealing of the front doorbell through the open door.

Everyone looked at each other as if to ask who was going to leave the comfort of their chair to go and see who would be inconsiderate enough to interrupt their lazy Sunday afternoon.

"I'm too tired to get up," Garrett moaned. "Rett kept me awake till all hours."

"Kept *you* awake?" Molly said, jabbing him with her elbow and eliciting a repentant yelp. "I was the one who gave him both feedings."

Cade closed his eyes. "I don't live here."

The bell rang a second time, and Shiloh heaved a great sigh. "I'll get it. I'd hate to disturb any of you lazy no accounts."

"Thanks, sis," Garrett said with a grin.

Shiloh rose and, passing the baby to Cade, flounced into the house with an air of injury. She was still smiling at the way she'd been manipulated by her brother as she turned the doorknob and flung the door wide. Her smile vanished like a UFO into the darkness of the night.

"Jack." She heard the quiver in her voice and hated herself for it.

"Hello, Shiloh," he said, giving her the benefit of that devilishly charming smile.

Shiloh didn't answer. Couldn't. Though she felt as if she was in a state of suspended animation, she noticed that he hadn't changed in the almost three months since she'd seen him. Or had he? Had that hint of arrogance always glittered in his eyes? Had those lines of dissipation always etched his lean cheeks?

Her heart beat out a tortured rhythm, not from pain or remorse. From anger. How dare he just...show up with a smile on his face, as if he hadn't ripped out her heart and thrown it—still beating in bloody anguish—at her feet. What on earth was he doing here? And how on earth had he tracked her down? She wasn't aware that she'd spoken the question out loud until he answered.

"I needed to talk to you, so I went to Le Mirage and had a little visit with Julie Scott. She let it slip that you'd visited your brother, and since I couldn't locate you anywhere else, I thought I'd fly down and check it out." Seeing the look on her face, he added, "Don't worry. She didn't betray your hiding place. I didn't let on that I wanted to look you up. I'm smarter than that."

Slick Jack strikes again. Shiloh didn't think Julie would deliberately squeal on her. "I'm not hiding, Jack. I'm starting a new life."

At the possibility that she might be able to survive without him, Jack's smile faded. "That easy, huh?"

"Easy?" Shiloh's lips twisted in a bitter mockery. "No. As a matter of fact, it's been hell."

His appraising glance moved over her from head to toe, taking in her bare legs with typical masculine appreciation. "It can't have been too hard on you. You look incredibly beautiful."

"You can stop dispensing the b.s., Jack," she told him in a sharp tone. "It's lost its allure. What made you decide to leave your safe little world and come down here?"

A look of humble remorse molded Jack's features. He shoved his hands into the pockets of his tailored slacks and lifted sorrowful eyes to hers. "I came because I made a mistake when I sent you and our baby away. I wanted to tell you that I'm sorry for the things I said, for the way I acted. I came because I've changed my mind. I want us to be a family. I want to do the right thing and marry you."

Shiloh was admiring the polish of Jack's performance and granting herself additional forgiveness for having fallen for his line when a deep voice said, "You were gone so long, I thought I'd see if something was wrong."

Both she and Jack turned toward the sound of Cade's voice. He stood a few feet away, Rett cradled in his arms. The look on his face told her without words that he'd heard Jack's magnanimous offer and knew exactly who he was.

"Nothing that I can't handle," she said. As Cade moved to her side, Rett upchucked all over his shirt. As if it were nothing, Cade handed her the baby, took the diaper from his shoulder, dabbed at Rett's mouth and began to wipe at the mess.

Jack grimaced in distaste. Shiloh counted her blessings.

Jack must have been doing some calculation of his own; he smiled. "This must be your brother."

"No, Jack," she said, taking malicious delight in the announcement, "this isn't my brother. This is my husband."

Even to Cade, the shock on Jack Delaney's face was comical. "Husband?" he echoed. "You're married?"

Shiloh nodded. "Almost two months now."

"Two months!" Jack exploded. The surprise on his face mutated to ugly fury. "So much for your undying love!" he spat. "You didn't waste any time, did you, you slut? Did you tell the Cajun here that you're pregnant with my baby, or did you plan to surprise him with a premature birth?"

Cade reached out and grabbed the front of Jack's shirt so fast that Shiloh would remember it later as just a blur. Jack never saw him move. All he saw was the icy anger in Cade's blue eyes.

"Let's step outside, you sorry son of a bitch, so I won't break any of my sister-in-law's antiques when I beat the hell out of you."

Shiloh grabbed his arm. "Cade, please."

He looked down at her, his mouth a tight line in his rigid face. "No one is going to talk about you like that."

"It doesn't matter," she said with a shake of her head. "I can handle this. Please."

Cade looked deep into her eyes for a moment. Then he released his punishing grip on the other man's shirt and smoothed the wrinkles with an exaggerated care that underscored his carefully leashed rage. With his jaw still clenched tightly, he took a step back.

"Thank you," she said, her eyes filled with gratitude and another emotion he was too upset to gauge. "Will you take the baby while I talk to Jack—alone?"

Cade cast Delaney a you-better-watch-it-buddy look and reached for Rett. "Sure."

Shiloh transferred her nephew to Cade's arms and turned toward the man who had fathered her child. "Let's go outside a minute, Jack," she said. "This won't take long."

Cade stopped pacing the hallway and looked at his watch. Ten minutes had passed since Shiloh and Jack had gone together down the wide steps that led to the flashy car parked in the circle driveway. Ten minutes that seemed like an eternity. Cade's heart felt full to bursting; it beat raggedly in his chest.

He knew she was right, that this was something she needed to take care of herself. She would be all right. Jack didn't look the type who'd get physical with a woman. But Cade knew his real fear wasn't for Shiloh's well-being. His real fear was for his—their—future.

His footsteps carried him to the living-room window that overlooked the garden where Molly, Garrett and the children still sat…waiting. Time, he thought. Time was what he and Shiloh needed. If only they'd had more time together, maybe the life he wanted for them would stand a better chance. But they didn't have time. All they had had together was one night, and despite the countless ways their bodies had communicated the message, there had been no words of love spoken. Would what they shared be forgotten in the rush of memories from her past?

There was no denying that Delaney was the type women seemed to go for. Smooth. Polished. Tan, with lots of golden-blond hair. Would seeing him make Shiloh realize that she loved him, after all? Why had he come now? Why not later—much later? Or never.

The sound of Jack's car peeling out of the shell driveway jolted Cade from his troubled thoughts. He heard Shiloh's steps on the porch, heard the screech of the screen door opening and the dull thud as it banged shut, heard it even over the loud beating of his heart. He turned to face her, dreading what she might say.

She looked composed. Not upset in the least. He couldn't read her, couldn't tell what she was thinking. "If you want out, I'll let you go," he said in a wooden voice.

"That makes twice you've offered to free me of this marriage," she said, her eyebrows drawn together in a frown. "Are you that anxious to get rid of me?"

It was only later that Cade would remember that she was supposed to have been asleep the other time, only later that they would laugh about all the misunderstandings.

"I'm not anxious to get rid of you. I'm offering you your freedom because I want you to be happy."

"Then let me stay," she begged, crossing the space separating them. Cade felt the tension in him ebb.

Sliding her arms around him, she pressed her cheek against his damp shirtfront. "You smell like expensive cologne and sour formula," she said, looking up at him, her nose wrinkled in that cute way he loved. "It becomes you."

He was afraid to trust the spark of hope that flickered inside him, unable to stop the burst of happiness. "I'll bet you say that to all the guys."

"Only if it's true," she said. Before he could reply, the tender light of love filled her eyes. "Let me grow old with you at Magnolia Manor," she begged. "Let me make crepes for you every Sunday morning. Love me the way you did last night for the rest of my life. Give me your baby. That's what will make me happy."

Cade felt his body tremble. He wanted to remember to thank God for Jack Delaney's stupidity. "Oh, God, *chère,* are you sure?"

Shiloh drew his head down until their mouths were a breath apart. "Very sure."

Epilogue

The May evening was heavy with the promise of summer. The temperatures had soared into the high nineties the past few days, and thunderstorms had plagued the area. The humidity was so high that Garrett claimed you could wring out the air. Cade said you might drown if you breathed in too deeply.

Shiloh stood at the downstairs window that overlooked Rambler's Rest's rose garden, watching her family and thanking God for second chances. Cade's kids had accepted her fully as a friend and sometime confidante, which is all she had ever dared to hope for.

Just now, Sunny was playing dolls with the lovely Laura Leigh, who was in hog heaven because the older girl was showering her with attention. Jared was deep in a discussion with his dad and Garrett, who was holding a wriggling Rett. Jared was such a handsome thing, she thought with typical motherly pride. *Both* of Cade's sons were exceptionally handsome.

Just as Ted Devane had said she could, she had indeed been able to get pregnant. Contrary to his predictions, it hadn't been hard at all. Actually, it had been easy. Maybe because Cade had made it such a pleasant and exciting task. Unlike her first experience, her pregnancy had been relatively trouble free, and Micah had been born on time after an easy labor. In the month since his birth he had slept and eaten on schedule, not bothering his parents with anything so annoying as colic or having his days and nights mixed up. He was perfect. Like his daddy.

As a compass needle is drawn to the north, Shiloh's gaze was drawn from the baby in his carrier to her husband seated a few feet away. He'd been working in the yard the past few days, and the sun had already started streaking his hair with golden highlights. He smiled at something Garrett said, and those crinkles she loved so much appeared in the corners of his eyes that looked bluer than blue against the tan of his face.

As if he sensed that someone was watching him, Cade looked up. Smiled. Shiloh's heart began to race in a familiar way. She would never get tired of looking at that face, she thought with a sudden surge of love that was almost painful. Not in a million, trillion years. He had been worth waiting for. Being loved by him had been worth waiting for.

"What are you doing?"

Shiloh turned. Molly, who had been squeezing lemons at the sink, was looking at her, a question in her eyes.

A dreamy smile curved Shiloh's lips. "Falling in love with my husband."

Ignoring Molly's puzzled expression, she went back to her vigil, finding Cade's loving gaze once more. It was true. Sometimes, like now, she looked at him and felt those fresh new feelings of love exploding inside her just as they had those long-ago summers when she'd visited her dad. Just as it had back then, breathlessness invaded her. Shyness took her captive. She felt fourteen again. Fourteen and hopelessly, helplessly in love. But this time there was a difference.

Now there was no fear.

*   *   *   *   *

Silhouette SPECIAL EDITION ™

It takes a very special man to win

That SPECIAL *Woman!*

She's friend, wife, mother—she's you! And beside each Special Woman stands a wonderfully *special* man. It's a celebration of our heroines— and the men who become part of their lives.

Look for these exciting titles from Silhouette Special Edition:

April   FALLING FOR RACHEL by Nora Roberts
Heroine: Rachel Stanislaski—a woman dedicated to her career discovers romance adds spice to life.

May   THE FOREVER NIGHT by Myrna Temte
Heroine: Ginny Bradford—a woman who thought she'd never love again finds the man of her dreams.

June   A WINTER'S ROSE by Erica Spindler
Heroine: Bently Cunningham—a woman with a blue-blooded background falls for one red-hot man.

July   KATE'S VOW by Sherryl Woods
Heroine: Kate Newton—a woman who viewed love as a mere fairy tale meets her own Prince Charming.

Don't miss THAT SPECIAL WOMAN! each month—from some of your special authors! Only from Silhouette Special Edition! And for the most special woman of all—you, our loyal reader—we have a wonderful gift: a beautiful journal to record all of your special moments. Look for details in this month's THAT SPECIAL WOMAN! title, available at your favorite retail outlet.

TSW2

Take 4 bestselling love stories FREE

Plus get a FREE surprise gift!

Special Limited-time Offer

Mail to Silhouette Reader Service™

3010 Walden Avenue
P.O. Box 1867
Buffalo, N.Y. 14269-1867

YES! Please send me 4 free Silhouette Special Edition® novels and my free surprise gift. Then send me 6 brand-new novels every month, which I will receive months before they appear in bookstores. Bill me at the low price of $2.71 each plus 25¢ delivery and applicable sales tax, if any.* That's the complete price and—compared to the cover prices of $3.50 each—quite a bargain! I understand that accepting the books and gift places me under no obligation ever to buy any books. I can always return a shipment and cancel at any time. Even if I never buy another book from Silhouette, the 4 free books and the surprise gift are mine to keep forever.

235 BPA AJH7

Name	(PLEASE PRINT)	
Address	Apt. No.	
City	State	Zip

This offer is limited to one order per household and not valid to present Silhouette Special Edition® subscribers. *Terms and prices are subject to change without notice. Sales tax applicable in N.Y.

USPED-93R

Silhouette SPECIAL EDITION®

MORGAN'S MERCENARIES

by
Lindsay McKenna

Morgan Trayhern has returned and he's set up a company full of best pals in adventure. Three men who've been to hell and back are about to fight the toughest battle of all . . . love!

You loved Wolf Harding in HEART OF THE WOLF (SE # 818), so be sure to catch the other two stories in this exciting trilogy. Sean Killian a.k.a. THE ROGUE (SE # 824) is coming your way in July. And in August it's COMMANDO (SE # 830) with hero Jake Randolph.

These are men you'll love and stories you'll treasure . . . only from Silhouette Special Edition!

Silhouette

SPECIAL EDITION®

From this day forward

Coming in August,
the first book in an exciting new trilogy from
Debbie Macomber
GROOM WANTED

To save the family business, Julia Conrad becomes a "green card" bride to brilliant chemist Aleksandr Berinski. But what more would it take to keep her prized employee—and new husband—happy?

FROM THIS DAY FORWARD—Three couples marry first and find love later in this heartwarming trilogy.

Look for
Bride Wanted (SE #836) in September
Marriage Wanted (SE #842) in October

Only from Silhouette Special Edition

SETD-1

by Laurie Paige

Come meet the wild McPherson men and see how these three sexy bachelors are tamed!

HOME FOR A WILD HEART, July 1993—
Kerrigan McPherson learns a lesson he'll never forget.

A PLACE FOR EAGLES, September 1993—
Keegan McPherson gets the surprise of his life.

THE WAY OF A MAN, November 1993—
Paul McPherson finally meets his match.

Don't miss any of these exciting titles—only for our readers and only from Silhouette Special Edition!

If you've been looking for something a little bit different and a little bit spooky, let Silhouette Books take you on a journey to the dark side of love with

Every month, Silhouette will bring you two romantic, spine-tingling Shadows novels, written by some of your favorite authors, such as *New York Times* bestselling author Heather Graham Pozzessere, Anne Stuart, Helen R. Myers and Rachel Lee—to name just a few.

In July, look for:
HEART OF THE BEAST by Carla Cassidy
DARK ENCHANTMENT by Jane Toombs

In August, look for:
A SILENCE OF DREAMS by Barbara Faith
THE SEVENTH NIGHT by Amanda Stevens

In September, look for:
FOOTSTEPS IN THE NIGHT by Lee Karr
WHAT WAITS BELOW by Jane Toombs

Come into the world of Shadows and prepare to tremble with fear—and passion....

SHAD3